CLAIMING HIS
DESIRE

FERAL BREED MOTORCYCLE CLUB
BOOK SIX

ELLIS LEIGH

Claiming His Desire
Copyright ©2015 by Ellis Leigh
All rights reserved
ISBN: 978-0-9961465-4-8

Kinship Press
P.O. Box 221
kinship press Prospect heights, IL 60070

*Dedicated to all of us blessed with second chances
and to those still waiting for theirs.*

ONE

Jameson

BLOOD STREAKED ACROSS MY plate, deep red on white, as I sliced through a hunk of meat. The scent of barely cooked flesh teased my senses—fresh, raw, and untainted. My mouth watered, and my inner wolf growled his pleasure. I may not have learned much in the century or so I'd been walking this earth, but I'd definitely learned how to prepare the perfect steak.

"Which bike are you riding tomorrow?"

I glared at Sandman, subtly hunching over my plate as my wolf snapped. Who interrupted a man during his meal? Not that I could work out my irritation with much more than a nasty look and a low growl. Sandman was acting as my mission partner while my regular sidekick, Shadow, was in Detroit getting mated up. Sandman was a cool enough guy, but he needed to learn the rules. You never get between a man and his steak. Especially not a man with an appetite as big as mine.

Fucking part-timer.

"The campground is, like, half a mile away," I finally said, stabbing a piece of meat and bringing it to my lips on the tip of my knife. "I might just walk it."

Sandman's eyes went wide for a second before he shook his head and chuckled. "Lying bastard."

"You walked into that one." I shrugged and grabbed the chunk off my knife with my teeth.

Oh hell, the moan I let out as the tangy, sweet flavor hit my tongue would have made a nice girl blush. I couldn't hold it in, though—my steak was the perfect taste and texture in one bite. I practically grew hard looking down at the rest of the meat on my plate.

"You taking the duck?"

I licked a drop of blood from my bottom lip, wishing Sandman wasn't so talkative. My dinner was way more important than his curiosity, but Blaze had made it clear that I needed to be nice until Shadow returned. If he returned. Shadow would probably end up kicked off our team, especially if he couldn't keep his head in the game. We had an important job to do, and there was no room for error. Especially not because a man was worried about the little woman back home. That was why mated shifters didn't ride—they lost their edge. Besides, Shadow's mate was a witch, practically a natural enemy of shifters. If word got out that he was *mated* to a witch? Forget it. His acceptance within our kind would be straight-up revoked and that would make him useless to this team. He'd end up alone within the breed, exiled, though he'd still have his mate by his side. That sort of bond couldn't be broken by ignorance and fear like the so-called bonds of friendship and pack. The mating bond would last no matter what happened. Even through the death of his mate, the gods forbid.

My gut clenched at that thought, memories of an old steel warehouse baking in the hot desert sun trying to fight their way through the wall I'd built in my mind. I snarled internally and pushed all that away. Steak, bikes, and hunting the fuckers messing with our Omegas. That was my life. That was all I wanted. That was what I needed to concentrate on. Not the almosts or the if onlys.

I wiped the back of my hand across my mouth, refusing to give in to the past. "I'm taking my H2R. I'm itching to burn up a few turns."

"Is that skid even street legal?"

My grin felt wide and wolfish, as it should be. My new Kawasaki was one badass ride. "Hell no."

Sandman took a bite of his chicken, focusing on the wall across from us as he chewed. "I can't imagine what happens when you and Shadow roll into a town."

"Why's that?"

"He's got that classic World War II XA and you've got the supercharged H2R. They're opposite sides of the spectrum in terms of style and can attract attention on their own. You two ride up at once, and you're a motorcycle lover's wet dream."

My laugh rumbled as I shook my head and stabbed another piece of steak. "Let's not ever talk about Shadow, me, and wet dreams in the same sentence again, okay, man?"

"Understood," Sandman replied, still laughing. "He's coming tomorrow, right?"

I nodded, chewing and swallowing another kick-ass bite of succulent meat. "Yeah, he's riding out with the Detroit and Kalamazoo dens in the morning."

Sandman glanced down, picking over his chicken and looking a little jealous as he eyed my slab of grass-fed beef. As he should. You don't go for chicken when there's steak available. And I sure as fuck wasn't sharing.

An image popped into my head, a dream I'd had, one of *her* biting into a hunk of something red and sweet, sighing, closing her eyes, licking her plump little lips. The kind of non-memory things that had been haunting me for a solid year. The pictures that made my stomach drop every time they forced their way into my mind.

"Do you think he's staying?" Sandman asked, yanking me

from the inevitable spiral of my thoughts. "Or will he retire to be with his mate?"

I gritted my teeth and stabbed another piece of meat, nearly cracking the plate. "I've spent the last year training with the guy. He'd better be fucking staying, but only if he can keep his priorities straight."

"His top priority will end up being his mate; that's the nature of our breed."

"And that's why mated shifters shouldn't ride with the Feral Breed." I shook my head, fighting back the rage bubbling inside of me, scattering pictures of dark hair and wide eyes to the recesses of my mind. This wasn't a conversation I wanted to have, nor was this a moment to have one of my delusional visions pop into my head. Especially not beside a man with the history and the intuitiveness of Sandman.

"Look," I said, slamming my knife down into another hunk. "If he wants to stay home and fuck her straight through the floor, good for him."

Dark hair tickling the length of my chest, pink lips wrapping around my cock, the way her hands would knead my hips as she took me all the way into her sweet mouth.

I swallowed hard, fighting for air. Fighting for clarity. "Let him focus on his little witch. But he'll have to drop off the team. We have Omegas to save, and no fated love connection can get in the way of that."

A smile, a whisper of my name in a feminine voice, the way her hands spread across my chest when she rode me, the way her touch made me crazy with need. Made me feel her love for me.

I closed my eyes and bit my lip hard enough to draw blood. Pain being the only thing that worked to yank me from my sad little not-quite-dreams. "I need a partner who's got my back and knows what's important here, not some love-struck kid who could get us all killed with his distractions."

Sandman sighed, finally meeting my eyes again. They slid

down to my lip, to the blood I could feel running down my chin, and filled with a look of pity that rankled. Hard.

"Don't," I growled, wiping my chin. "I'm trying to enjoy my dinner."

"I just… I understand why this gets to you so much."

I laughed, harsh and loud as my heart cracked. "You understand jack shit. Leave it."

Sandman nodded and looked away. "You know, one of these days—"

The sound of a feminine giggle interrupted whatever bullshit he was about to say and had us both turning toward the entrance to the kitchen. Blaze, the honoree of tomorrow's ride and the president of the NALB, came strolling through the door with his mate tucked under his arm. Well, one of his mates. The man had two.

"Good evening, gentlemen," Blaze said with a huge grin on his face. I pushed back the bile building within me and gave him a tight smile and a head nod.

"Evening, sir," I bit out.

"Nice to see you again, sir." Sandman stood, glancing from Blaze to Moira with a look of almost wistfulness on his face. I understood that look…way more than most people would have believed. Not that I'd show it. I couldn't have the whole Feral Breed crew thinking I'd gone soft or feeling sorry for my ass. It was bad enough Sandman knew a little about my situation. Nosy fucker.

"We were just coming to grab a snack," Moira said, her face a little flushed. She looked happy, which just set my gut to churning again.

Tears on pale skin, those wide eyes I could never unsee rimmed in red. Her hands reaching for me as the distance between us grew.

Blaze's smile turned wolfish. "My lovely mate here was feeling a bit peckish. She and Dante were—"

Moira smacked his arm, giggling again. "Blasius Zenne, you

hush." She turned our way, shrugging. "We were celebrating his birthday."

"Ah," Sandman said. "Well, please, don't let us be in your way. We were just having a late dinner."

I grabbed my plate and headed for the sink, too heartsick to finish my meal. "Yeah, go wild. I'm done here anyway."

I scraped the rest of my steak into the trash and washed the plate in the stainless steel sink. Even though there was staff to clean up after us, I couldn't help but take care of myself. I'd been washing my own plates since I was just a pup; I certainly wasn't going to stop now just because I was staying in some rich man's house. Hiding from my own life.

With a final nod to the happy couple, I stormed down the back hall and headed for my room. I needed a break, to settle in and refocus my thoughts on the job at hand. I needed to let go of what would never come to be. I'd missed my shot. The visions needed to either push me over the edge, finally make me go insane and become a man-eater so my brothers could end me, or get the fuck out of my head. A year was a long time to be stuck in this kind of purgatory.

Sadly, based on the heavy footsteps echoing mine, Sandman had decided following me was a good idea. The pushy son of a bitch should know better.

"Jameson, wait."

I stopped, feet planted shoulder-width apart, a low growl rumbling through me as my fingertips lengthened into claws. "I don't want to talk right now, man."

"I know," he said as he stood behind me, not challenging in any way, staying submissive and almost hiding behind my back to help calm my rage. As if there was any way to avoid the tornado of emotion swirling within me. "I've been there, pushing it down, drowning in it. But you have to let those feelings out or—"

I spun, my growl turning to a snarl, my jaw cracking as the

bones began to re-form into a muzzle. "Or what? They'll eat me alive? Put me in an early grave? Drive me fucking crazy and take away what little control over my wolf I have left?"

Sandman stood tall, head up, eyes on mine. "Exactly. You'll become a man-eater, and we'll have to put you down."

"Good," I spat before turning and walking away. "I've been fucking waiting for that day."

I ignored his calls, slamming the door to my room once I stalked inside. Snarling and suffering as my body shifted between forms slowly, I used all my energy to hold myself together. Stay human. Fight back my beast.

Fucking Sandman. The bastard had killed the calm I'd been trying to achieve, igniting my temper with only a handful of words. I paced the small room I'd claimed as my own in the rear of the basement. No one else stayed back here, at least not voluntarily. There were always a handful of shifters in cages in the lower basement level—the one most people never knew about—but the good little boy and girl shifters who came to Merriweather Fields preferred to live upstairs in the more modern and cushy accommodations offered to the staff.

I didn't want cushy.

I wanted dark and dank, quiet and alone. A den to hole up in and hide. A place to die over and over again without drawing attention from the gossipmongers upstairs. Sandman worried about me finding an early grave, but I looked forward to it.

A hand pulling her long hair off her face, her teeth white as she bit her lip, concentrating on what she was reading. Alive, real, beside me.

I whimpered and curled into a ball on the concrete floor, tucking myself in the corner. She wasn't real; the visions weren't real. And yet they haunted me. Tortured me.

Because she should have been mine.

The mate the fates had given me—the woman I'd only seen from a distance one time before she invaded every moment of my day through false memories and impossible visions—was dead. Had been since the moment I spotted her. So the fact that I knew her smell, her taste, and the warmth of her touch was utterly and completely impossible.

And yet my mind played tricks on me, making me uncertain what was reality anymore. Making me wish for death. Because the sooner I joined her, the sooner I could stop the raging agony inside of me. Maybe. If death led me to anywhere other than hell, or if I was lucky.

I huffed a laugh that turned into another whine.

Since when had I ever been lucky?

I AVOIDED SANDMAN FOR as long as possible the next morning, too groggy from my night spent on the floor, my nerves too frayed by the torturous delusions to deal with his shit. But being that we were both heading to the same place for the same reason, dodging Sandman was a temporary solution at best.

"Sleep okay?" Sandman asked as he joined me in the library. I raised an eyebrow and grunted before returning to study the map of the grounds spread across a desk.

"Be prepared for a water evac," Bez, one of the Cleaners assigned to the case of the missing Omegas said, running a finger down the river at the eastern edge of the property. "There are tunnels that lead under the cemetery here—" he stabbed one spot with his blunt finger "—and they come out over here." Another spot, this one over the map of the house itself. In fact, a spot awfully close to the room I'd been staying in. I'd never seen a tunnel access point back there, but that didn't mean it didn't exist. If Bez said the tunnel started by my room, then it did. The fucker was as reliable as the sun.

Her face turned up, bathed in the pink light of a desert sunset, her smile soft and kind.

I huffed, biting my lip again. Using pain to ground me in the now. In what was real and urgent, not giving in to the pull of my dreams.

"The safe room in the president's private quarters is ready, and the one in the basement is being restocked as a backup." Bez glanced around the room, his ice-blue eyes spearing each of us in turn. "Be prepared. Be watchful. Be ready. We haven't heard any grumblings about the celebration, but you can never let silence allow you to become complacent. We'll head out in teams later this morning to canvass the campground where the carnival will be held."

I glanced at Sandman, who had his arms crossed over his chest and a serious expression on his face as he watched me. Fuck, I had to hang with him the entire day. As my stand-in partner, he would be monitoring and patrolling Blaze's birthday carnival by my side. Probably giving me that pitiful, understanding look. The one that said, "I know how you feel." Too bad the guy had no clue how I felt, how I'd been feeling since the day I spotted my mate lying still and gray across a concrete floor. Dead, green eyes open and staring, seeing nothing as the bond between us made itself known in the most perverse way.

Her eyes on mine as I bit along her hipbone, as I spread her legs and tasted her most secret flesh, as I slid my tongue inside.

Guilt and shame sat in my stomach like a lead ball, making me sick. That day, the day I found her body, had been the beginning of the end for me. I'd grown hard just looking at her cold, dead body. I hadn't even been able to walk into the warehouse and do the job Blaze had ordered me to because of it. Pain and disgust had flooded me as my lust soared, made me hate myself even as my mind filled with every naughty thing I'd wanted to do to her. But she was dead, so I ran. I'd grabbed my bike and driven north, out of the city and away from that scene. Been running ever since. I let my old Feral Breed den clean up my mess and headed straight for Blaze to be reassigned. No way could I stay in the desert, not after that.

Scrubbing a hand over my face, I glared at Sandman. For whatever reason, he'd taken it upon himself to "heal" me once he figured out my mate had died. As if that were possible. He was too open, too honest, and way too fucking smart to be around me for much longer. Bad enough I'd lost my mate, if he found out how I'd gotten turned on by the sight of her dead body? How I'd run like a bitch and left her corpse behind? His pity would turn to disgust, as it should. I needed to get Shadow off his witch and back to work. At least he didn't know about my mate or my disgusting mistakes. He was a bright kid, but he had nothing on an aged shifter like Sandman.

As the meeting broke apart and the room emptied, Sandman came to my side. Cautious. Nonthreatening. Smart.

"Hey, I wanted to apologize for what I said," he began, looking to all the world like a man without an agenda. Something I doubted. "It's not my business, and I shouldn't push you so much."

"True facts." I coughed, the hoarseness in my voice making me uncomfortable. "It's good, man. Just back off, all right? I don't…want to talk about all that. Ever."

"Right. Understood." Sandman nodded. "Want to grab an early lunch before we head over to the campground?"

I shrugged, my stomach rumbling. I'd had steak and eggs for breakfast, but that had been a couple hours ago. "Could eat."

We left the room together, though silent. Each caught up in our own thoughts. My mind had been spinning all morning, taking me back to that day. To her. Hell, I'd dreamed of her all night, some dreams good, some really good. Her smile, her laugh, the way she would have touched me, would have looked at me with love in her eyes. The way her skin would have felt under my fingers and against my lips.

As had happened every morning since that day in the desert, I'd woken up hard and aching for her, my cock practically screaming for release. And just like every morning, I'd jacked off in the shower to the image of her, guilt making my stomach sour. She was killing me, slowly burying me in a need I couldn't fulfill and a guilt I couldn't let go. I wished someone would hurry up and dump a bulldozer load of both on me so I could end it all. Be with her in the only way left available to me. In death.

But as we stepped into the hallway leading to the basement kitchens, the quiet shattered, an explosion blasting from the front of the mansion and making the entire building tremble with the force. In less than a second, the hall filled with Cleaners and Merriweather security guards, all hurrying to their posts. Bez appeared almost out of nowhere, stalking from the private residences. His face and gait filled with a rage I'd never seen, one that promised imminent death to whoever had dared to bring a fight to our door.

"I want every access point guarded. Spread out to your positions, guards," he yelled. "Levi, Mammon, and Thaus are already securing the president. Our job is to keep those fuckers who thought they could blow up our goddamned home on the other side of the doors. Jameson, I want you with me at the front of the house. Now."

Sandman and I rushed toward the east entrance, weaving through the crowd of guards storming down the hall. I slid to a stop in front of one of the many windows along the main floor, the sight before me making my inner wolf spring up with a snarl. He didn't like to be challenged, and a challenge was what he saw happening outside.

A line of shifters surrounded the property, spreading out as far as I could see.

"Motherfuckers," I whispered. "They brought their whole damn clan with them."

Sandman blew out a breath, the sound rumbling with his growl. "What do we do?"

"We fight," Bez replied, sliding up behind us, his growl turning fierce as he glared out the window. "We protect the president and his mates, the primary targets of any attack. To do so we need to fortify the presidential residence and prepare all who are in Merriweather for battle. That is our mission."

"We have guests here." Sandman circled the room, looking out each and every window in turn. "The pack Alphas, their mates, children, the Regional Heads...all the guests who came out for Blaze's birthday celebration. We've got hundreds more headed this way, and not all of them can go up against this kind of threat. Hell, even your mate and ward are around here somewhere. Sariel could maybe fight, but Angelita's just a pup. She's not ready for this."

Bez snarled, an unusual quicksilver swirling through the icy blue of his eyes. "Don't think I don't already know that, boy."

"Then we need more of a plan than just protecting the president and his mates." I glanced through another window. "Damn, that line doesn't seem to end. How many do you think are out there?"

"Too many." Bez grabbed his phone and pressed a few buttons. He held it out before him as a voice came over the speaker, uttering a single, clipped word.

"Situation?"

"Merriweather is under attack, and we appear to be outnumbered. Send an SOS call to the Regional Heads and the Feral Breed crews...now."

TWO

Aoife

THE VAN SLID INTO a curve, rising up on two wheels and throwing me into the door. I grabbed the oh-shit handle and tried to right myself, failing miserably. Percy cursed and pumped the brakes as we crashed back down, the force making me almost slide out of my seat belt.

"We have to hurry," I hissed, rubbing my head where it had knocked against the side window.

"I'm driving as fast as I can, Aoife. This bucket of rust isn't going to magically move any faster just because we want it to."

I shot a glare his way, though it fell as soon as I saw the bags under his eyes. We'd been driving for two solid days, screaming up from southern Arizona to western Michigan without stopping, all because of a dream he'd had. A dream of death, destruction, and great loss for a group of witches we'd never met by an enemy he couldn't quite see. I'd say it seemed odd, but in our lives, not so much.

"We're close," I said, fighting against the pull drawing me in a different direction. One that felt familiar and yet new at the same time, comforting and yet something I'd been resisting for months. A need that grew louder and more real the farther north we came.

"A mile or less is my guess," Percy said, his voice low and controlled. That tone was a sure sign he was looking ahead, using his gift to see the future and plan our path. I'd heard that distracted, businesslike edge to his voice since we were little kids growing up in the same foster home. I'd known the cause of it almost since we first met, from the moment we realized we were both the same—too different from normal folks to be accepted. So we'd accepted each other. A precog and a necromancer. One surrounded by the past, by death and loss, and one playing with the future, seeing what had yet to come.

I hissed as we hurtled north, the pull inside of me squeezing tighter. It dragged at my soul, demanding I head somewhere else, making me need something I couldn't quite identify. Or someone, really.

"Where?" Percy asked, not needing me to explain what was wrong. As usual. He'd been with me since I felt the pull the first time. He knew how much it pained me, how much I ached from it at times.

"West. South and west. We passed it."

"Let's make sure these witches survive to see tomorrow, and then we'll go hunting down the bastard torturing you." Percy gripped the wheel as he made yet another turn, this time keeping all four wheels on the dirt road.

"He's not torturing me." I frowned, tasting what was almost a lie as I stared out the window to the west. Watching for a lighthouse. Trying not to think about what lay out there that could be calling me, that had the strength to spend a year making me yearn. That could create such a desire within me.

Percy huffed and turned onto an even smaller road, obviously knowing where we needed to be. "Could have fooled me."

I closed my eyes as the pain increased, my mind immediately flooded with images of blue eyes and wild, blondish hair. Of muscles, tattoos, and an expression of rage that melted into one of utter horror. Of a man I'd know anywhere but had never met. A man who'd starred in every naughty fantasy I'd had over the past year, and even some not-so-naughty ones.

A man who'd taken one look at me and run the other way.

"Get ready," Percy said, interrupting my thoughts. I crawled out of the seat and grabbed my compound bow and a backpack full of arrows from the back of the van. Being a necromancer had its perks—though they were few and far between—but having any kind of fighting ability wasn't one of them. In high school, I'd joined the archery team after the spirit of a woman whose grave I happened across told me I'd like the sport. She'd been right. Not only did I like it, I was good at it. Good enough to be willing to rush into a fight that wasn't my own to save a coven of witches from being burned alive. A fate Percy had been forced to watch over and over as we headed north.

Percy's gift was much less of a gift and more of a horror movie some days.

"There," I said as the top of a white and black lighthouse peeked above the trees. Percy didn't pause, turning the wheel hard and sending us hurtling down a sand and grass driveway of sorts. I grabbed the seat in front of me and held on as the van jostled and rumbled toward the shore of Lake Michigan.

"Holy shit."

I had no idea which of us whispered the exclamation, maybe both. The scene we rolled up on as we came around the final curve was one I'd never even thought to imagine.

"Are those—" Percy paused and licked his lips, his eyes wide "—are they wolves?"

"They're too big to be wolves. Werewolves?"

"We've dealt with werewolves before, so I can see them in my visions. These are new. Besides, it's morning. Wouldn't werewolves be human again?"

I shrugged. "Who knows anymore? Between running into

werewolves outside Phoenix and dealing with those vampires in Flagstaff, I'm on a paranormal overload. Let's just hope they die like regular animals do."

Percy nodded and sighed. "Here's to hoping."

He jumped into the back as I slid the side door open and crawled onto the roof of the van, staying close to my supply of arrows in case the twenty in my backpack weren't enough. The carnage was even more horrific from up there. Wolves fought in the clearing that led to the beach, claws and teeth tearing through flesh, blood splattering the grass and painting what should have been green a rusty brown. A small group of women lined the porch on the lake side of the lighthouse, looking on in fear and disbelief. The witches, I presumed.

"They need to get away from the building," Percy yelled, pointing at the women. "I still see the place going up in flames. I'll run while the dogs are distracted. You cover me."

"You'd better run fast." I raised my arm and notched an arrow, loading it, not yet drawing the bow, watching the pack of animals killing each other. "I have no idea which are the good wolves and which are the bad."

"They all look like big, bad wolves to me," Percy said before he jumped out of the van and sprinted for the lighthouse.

"No shit," I whispered, drawing the bow to my cheek, aiming into the fray as I kept Percy in my peripheral vision. Good or bad, if a wolf approached him, I'd shoot. He was my best friend and the only family I had...no canine boogeyman was going to take him down while I watched. Luckily, Percy made it to the porch unnoticed before the weight of the draw became too much for me; the wolves were too busy fighting each other to bother with what they probably saw as a lowly human. If only they knew.

As Percy spoke to the women, I kept an arrow ready in my bow and my eyes trained on the wolves. A large, black one fought like a demon released, tearing through the lineup of grays and browns with a smaller, pure white wolf by his side. Something about them spoke to me, some kind of energy on the air telling me they were the good guys. The ones to protect. Though by the way the black ripped the heads off some of the other wolves, it wouldn't have surprised me to find out he was the worst of the bunch. He definitely seemed the most dangerous.

As the fighting increased, growls and snarls filling the air, I watched. Waited. Kept my bow notched and my eyes on the fight until—

"Save the white!"

Percy's yell was all I needed. I drew my bow to my cheek, aiming at a large, gray wolf heading toward the white one, sending my arrow soaring through the air and into his chest. The beast fell to the side, his paws scrabbling in the dirt, blood pooling on the grass. Again and again, I nocked, drew, and released my arrows, keeping all but the black away from the white, somehow sensing that their connection was a positive one. That the black was fighting for the white in this battle.

I aimed for a tan wolf that was circling the white, ready to shoot, but a gray jumped out and knocked the lighter wolf down before I got the chance.

"No!" Percy's scream again caught my attention, though I had no idea which animal he was screaming about. Staying our original course, I kept the white wolf in my sights, knocking out those that approached it as fast as I could. Cutting through the attackers with speed and precision born of hours spent on the target range instead of doing normal things like finishing school or finding a job. The dead didn't really understand the concept of do-not-disturb time.

Suddenly, two of the gray wolves were no longer wolves. They were men…naked, human men. And they looked really pissed about something as they glared at the black wolf.

"The King will skin you alive, Gatekeeper."

The black wolf shifted human, standing naked and holy-hell-glorious. No man should be that pretty, especially not one who could turn into an overgrown dog and decapitate his fellow wolf-men with a single slice. Bathed in blood and surrounded by an aura of rage, he captivated me. I couldn't look away. But to be honest, rage looked good on him.

"You tell your so-called King I win again. Next time he sends someone for my mate, it'll be *his* head I come after." The man stalked forward, aggressive and fierce. The grays smirked and held their ground. Waiting him out, which seemed like a bad idea to me. Another man, one I assumed was with the grays, appeared behind them, slinking from the tree line with something in his hand.

"You dare to threaten our King while you wallow with the impure and the mutts?" the new man said, sneering at the one they'd called Gatekeeper. "We came to teach you a lesson today. You and a few of your friends."

Gatekeeper opened his arms, indicating the fallen wolves on the ground. "Looks like you're the ones learning a lesson today."

The other man made a noise like a growl, his face twisting in anger. "The King wants your crew to know that, when he replaces Blasius Zenne as leader of the National Association of the Lycan Brotherhood, any wolf daring to mate outside our breed will be banished, if not executed. You make sure to tell your Feral Breed denmates. Humans will be tolerated, but the witches will be burned at the stake as they deserve."

I kept my bow up, ready to draw and release, even as I glanced Percy's way. His eyes were locked on the man speaking, a nervous edge to his body. He'd managed to move the witches off the porch but was still awfully close to the lighthouse. A position that seemed dangerous to me.

"You come after any one of our mates, and the whole of the Feral Breed will be hunting your ass down." Gatekeeper snarled loudly, twisting his neck in a very nonhuman way to make his point.

The man smiled wickedly, a look filled with malice, before he did some kind of half bow thing. "Good luck, Gatekeeper. We'll see you again *real soon*." With that, the man tossed something toward the lighthouse, shifting into a wolf and running north with his two buddies hot on his heels.

Gatekeeper stepped as if to follow, but a blast at the base of the building nearly knocked him off his feet. The home attached to the actual lighthouse crumbled in place, the entire structure going up in flames as I watched. Thankfully, Percy and the witches weren't close enough to be in danger. They all stood on the safe side, watching as what I had to assume was their home burned.

"You good, Aoife?" Percy yelled, leading the witches toward the lake.

I nodded and held up my bow. "Made it through. You okay over there?"

"All good."

The Gatekeeper—sadly, no longer naked but wearing some kind of cape—approached the van. Growling. Wary. The white wolf walked by his side, brushing his legs every step. The two connected, and not just physically. Something in their auras seemed linked as well. Something I'd never seen before.

Another man walked behind them, also wary, his red hair gleaming in the sun.

"Who are you?" the red-haired man demanded, his voice harsh and aggressive. Too bad for him, I'd seen worse, heard worse, and lived through worse. A little mean tone to the voice wasn't going to get my heart racing by any stretch.

I huffed through my nose, matching his tone with one of my own. "I'm Aoife. And that's Percy."

He stared at me, stalking closer, the energy around him completely combative. "What are you doing here?"

Okay, that got my temper up. After two days on the road and watching Percy get sick every time he had to see the end of his vision, I had no patience for some man to question me. Jumping down from the roof, I gave him my best bitch glare and kept my voice flat, deadpan. Sarcastic as hell.

"*I'm* keeping the witches from being burned alive, not that you seem to want to say thank you for that. What are *you* doing here, wolf-man?"

He looked surprised, eyes wide and head jerking back. As if no one had ever questioned him before, as if everyone had simply bowed to his will. But it was the darker man who answered, his tone fierce and rightly so.

"We were saving my mate."

I lowered my bow and shook out my hands, my arms a little numb. "The white wolf? Yeah, good thing Percy yelled to me. I wasn't sure for a minute there who to aim for."

Suddenly, the white wolf transformed into a beautiful blonde. A naked one pretty enough to compete with Gatekeeper.

"Gates," she said, her tone urgent. "Numbers was hit."

All three wolf-people turned, hurrying toward a fallen tan wolf across the grass. One I knew was past being helped. Death hung heavy in the air, circling the bodies, gleeful in his bounty. He hovered over the tan wolf, telling me his life was over, that whoever he had been no longer mattered. The spirit of the man beneath the fur would leave this plane within moments, heading to the land of the dead...hopefully.

Percy stood beside me, watching the same scene but with different eyes. Ones that couldn't see the specter of Death but could see what was about to happen. And how it would affect me.

"You wish those boys were still naked, don't you?" he whispered, touching my arm, grounding me.

I rolled my eyes, seeing through his distraction attempt but following along anyway. Percy knew how hard fresh death could be on me. He'd seen me after the vampire attack at the warehouse in Flagstaff.

So had the man with the blue eyes.

I shoved off the memory of that day, of those eyes piercing my soul from across the room, and refocused on the scene before me. Playing along with Percy as a way to avoid what I knew was coming.

"Like you don't." Other images rolled through my mind, fake memories, scenes that had dogged me since that day in the desert. Of the tattooed man naked and above me, of the way his body would look in the early-morning sun, how each and every curve of his muscles would appear deeper, stronger, shadows adding depth to his form. The man made my knees weak and he only lived in my dreams…for the moment.

Percy shoved me, catching me off guard and almost knocking me over with a grin on his face. "Oh, baby girl, I definitely do. I could stare at that all day."

"You're such a naughty little thing. I think that's why we're friends."

"There's no shame in being honest." He shrugged, purposely casual, this game one we'd played a hundred times before. "The girl is nice to look at, too. If you're into that kind of thing."

I scoffed but then went quiet, watching, trying to be respectful. The two men knelt beside the fallen wolf, mourning. The woman—having donned a cloak of her own—stood behind the darker one, hand on his shoulder, supporting him in a subtle, quiet way that tugged at my heart. I hated watching people display their grief, couldn't stand the rawness of it when death was such an everyday occurrence for me. Their pain made me feel broken, heartless, and wrong because I experienced none of it. All I felt was the weight of responsibility my gift gave me and the need to make sure the spirit of the fallen found their way home.

I tried to turn, to wait for the soul of the fallen wolf

22   *Claiming His Desire*

somewhere I couldn't see his body, but the red-haired man caught my attention. He'd taken a knee, bowed his head, and knelt next to the wolf's body, seeming to pray. The image hit me hard, a man who'd shown such aggression appearing so broken. After a moment of silence, he slid his arms under the wolf's body and lifted the tan fur-covered body against his chest.

"What's he doing?" Percy asked, watching the man walk toward the lighthouse, carrying his load as if it was something precious and delicate.

"I don't know. You're the one who knows all."

Percy huffed. "Most. I know most, not all. And for this, I know nothing. I'm still a little foggy when it comes to these wolf-men. Though there's a lovely witch named Amber I believe I need to find."

"For what?" I asked, having never heard him mention an Amber before. Percy shrugged but didn't answer, staring off across the field instead.

The witches moved to create a semicircle around the back of the man as he approached the burning lighthouse. Sirens sounded in the distance, but he paid them no mind. He simply nodded his head to his fallen comrade one last time before tossing the wolf into the burning building.

"Cremation," Percy whispered, still staring. "Does that mean—"

"Yep," I said, bracing myself. "Eviction notice officially served. This is going to suck for me." Before I could take a step back, the soul of the man who'd resided within the dead beast flew at me. Eyes wide, his scream piercing the air, he appeared exactly like what he kind of was—a man on fire.

"Tell him," he screamed, making me flinch. "Tell Gates to get moving. My death isn't important, but Blaze's would be."

I stumbled back, no longer seeing the world around me, too consumed by the smoky wisps that made up his form. "I don't know—"

"Tell him." His scream interrupted what I wanted to say, scattering my thoughts and scrambling my brain waves. I gripped my head, trying and failing to protect myself from his screeching. Fuck, the newly dead were loud.

"Okay, okay." I held my hands up, practically bent in half to avoid him. "Percy?"

"I'm here," he answered, his anxiety clear.

"I need to talk to the wolf-men. Right now."

"On it." Percy grabbed my arm and pulled me, giving me enough slack to dodge the smoky substance that made up the spirit in this plane, and rushed me across the grass.

The dark-haired man was closest, and I lunged for him. "He said you need to go."

All three of the wolves-in-human-clothes turned to face me, but it was the dark-haired one who approached. The one they'd called Gatekeeper, all bright eyes and bad attitude in a fuckhot package.

"What did you say?"

"The guy…inside the wolf." I hooked a thumb in the direction of the fire where the body burned. "He said you need to get moving. His death isn't important."

"Look," Gates growled, obviously a little pissed off. "I don't know who you are—"

The spirit screamed again, making it hard to hear. Hell, he made it hard to think even as his essence faded, as he began his transition to the land of the dead. Feeling rushed, giving up all sense of manners, I barreled over whatever tall, dark, and crabby wanted to say.

"I'm sure you're going to tell me how I'm rude and you need to mourn you friend," I said, probably yelling at him but having a hard time dealing with the spirit due to his lack of volume control. "But the guy—Numbers. Yes, I got it, your name is Numbers—says to get moving. Something about Blaze's death being more important that his. Can you stop screaming at me, dude?"

Gates stared, his eyes locked on mine. I didn't waver, didn't shy away from that inspection. Let him look—I knew I was telling the truth. Finally, he gave me a chin bob, a move I assumed meant he'd accepted my story.

"Time to go," Gates said, peering out over the lake. "We're needed at Merriweather."

The redhead's eyes went wide. "You're just going to buy her story? Numbers is dead...he couldn't have told her anything."

Percy smirked. "She's a necromancer, so yeah, he could. Get used to it."

Before anyone could answer, the witches approached, all appearing tired and overwhelmed. The spirit of Numbers faded in their presence, his voice softening. I silently wished him peace in his afterlife, sensing the passing of his soul from this plane to the next.

"Thank you both for coming." The witch I guessed was the leader looked over each of us in turn before turning to Percy and me. "We appreciate your sacrifices to help us avoid such a disaster. This coven has seen enough loss lately."

I glanced at Percy. "But we didn't save the house—"

"Houses can be rebuilt," the witch interrupted. "Our family is irreplaceable. So, thank you."

Percy nodded. "Glad to have seen the problems and been able to intervene."

She faced the one called Gates, frowning, her eyes sad. "I'm very sorry for the loss of your friend. We will perform a cleansing ritual for him before sunset to show our respect."

He bowed as he muttered a soft "Thank you."

She paused, staring at him. "You look very much like a man who helped us in the fall."

Gates stood to his full height, looking respectful and even kind. "My brother, Beast, was here with a man named Phoenix. Your former covenmate, Azurine, met them not too far from here along with Scarlett. Beast helped the girls move to Detroit and put Scarlett and Amber up in his home for a while."

"Ah yes, that's it," she said with a nod and a small smile, one tinged with a sadness equal to that of the wolves who'd lost their friend. "And how are the Weavers doing? We've missed them greatly."

"They're well," the blond woman interjected, eyeing Gates hard. "Brokenhearted to have been kicked out of their own family and home, but finding new lives and friends."

The witch's smile fell, and a deep look of regret flashed in her eyes. "We did not understand the situation when we banished Azurine. If we had, we never—"

"I apologize, but we really have to go," Gates said as the sirens grew closer. "Ladies, I'm going to have to ask you to clean up the mess to help us all. If you could burn the bodies so the humans can't get their hands on them, that would be best."

"Of course," one of the witches said. "Please let the Weavers know of the damage to the lighthouse. This was their home, too."

"I will." Gates nodded once, his eyes darting toward the road. "Do you happen to have a vehicle we can borrow? Kaija, Klutch, and I are needed in Chicago."

The single word—Chicago—hit me like a physical force. I jerked, gasping, my heart racing.

"Yes, Chicago." I looked to Percy, feeling how wide my eyes had grown, struggling to make myself clear. "I need to go to Chicago."

Percy watched me, his face wary. "The blue-eyed guy?"

"Yeah." I shook off the pull, rubbing at my chest to ease the pain inside. "He's in Chicago. Or close to it."

"So we're off to Chicago." Percy nodded once, then turned back to the wolves. "Need a lift?"

Gates blinked. "Seriously?"

"Yeah, why not?" Percy shrugged as he headed for the van.

"Besides, I'm pretty sure we're all going to the same place."

"Doubtful," the red-haired man, Klutch, I assumed, muttered.

"Don't doubt a seer," I spat. "Percy knows more about the future than any of us could even guess at. If he thinks our paths are converging, then you can bet they are."

Klutch looked from Percy to me and back before sighing. "My apologies for the assumption."

"Accepted, Klutch…right?" I held out my hand, shaking his as he nodded. "I'm very sorry for your loss."

His eyes darted to mine, wide with surprise. The blond woman next to him smiled and reached for my proffered hand.

"I'm Kaija, and Gates over there is my mate. I wish I could say it's nice to meet you, but—"

"Circumstances." I nodded, frowning. "I understand you're mourning, but we're in a time crunch. How about we hop inside the van so we can get on the road before the cops show up?"

"Yeah, that sounds like a good idea." She stepped into the van with ease, immediately moving into the far back of the cargo area. I followed her, pausing just inside the door, watching as the witches scattered across the field. Within moments, bodies disappeared into ash, the magic of the witches burning the shells from this plane and sending the spirits soaring. Thankfully, not in my direction.

"May you find your peace," I whispered as Gates slammed the sliding door of the van closed.

"The only wolf out there deserving your prayers is Numbers," he growled, his eyes hard when they met mine. "If the rest wanted peace, they shouldn't have become criminals."

My stomach twisted into a knot. "Everyone makes mistakes, Gates. Sometimes, they just need a little boost to help them break free from a bad situation and clean up their act."

Kaija watched our interaction with interest. Her pale eyes

almost hunted me, the animal energy around her making me want to retreat. Instead, I stared right back. Waiting her out. Refusing to back down.

"Perhaps you're right, Aoife the necromancer." Kaija tilted her head, the move animalistic and predator-like. "I have my doubts, but stranger things have happened."

"Like watching men and women change into wolves?"

"Or watching a simple arrow take down creatures that regenerate fast enough to beat most causes of death." She leaned forward, pinning me with her eyes. "What's your secret?"

I shrugged, refusing to look away. Tucking my secret down deep inside. "No one beats Death forever."

THREE

Jameson

"IN YOU GO." I grabbed the arm of a human woman holding an infant and helped her over the safe room threshold. She seemed familiar to me, but without asking or sniffing her to figure out who her mate was—which she might think was rude—I couldn't quite place her. Still, I felt for her and whoever fathered her little one. That baby shouldn't have been here. This was not the situation for someone so fragile.

"Do you know where the others are?" the woman asked, leaning toward me. Looking as if she knew me.

"What others?"

Her brow furrowed before she frowned, seeming to realize I had no idea who she was. "The other women from the Detroit Feral Breed den. I'm Beast's mate, Calla. We met once at the denhouse there. Charlotte, Zuri, Scarlett... They were going to the campground for a final walk-through with a few others, and I didn't know if they'd gotten back when the explosion went off."

My stomach sank even as I schooled my face into a mask of what I hoped was calm. *Damn it...*two of those women were witches, not a high priority in the minds of shifters who tended to have an almost automatic negative response to the little magic-throwers. They could probably fight back against a shifter or two if need be, but Rebel's mate, Charlotte, was human. She'd be a sitting duck outside the house.

Green eyes…dead eyes…staring at me from across a warehouse. Blood all around her. The scent of vampire lingering…

"Don't worry," I said, keeping my voice soft and quiet. "I'll make sure someone tracks them down. They may just be in the other safe room upstairs."

"Okay." She frowned harder, not looking at all convinced. "Maybe you're right. But please, check? I'm worried about them."

"I'll check." I made to leave, but she grabbed my arm, stopping me.

"Promise me?"

I took a step back and yanked my arm from her hold. "I'm not a liar."

"No, I never said that." She moved closer again, a strength burning deep inside her I hadn't noticed before. "But you are a shifter. As much as I love my mate and am friendly with his denmates, I don't trust your kind easily. Those girls are family; I need to know they're safe."

Before I could answer her, Sandman led two human women and a young shifter inside the safe room, forcing me to take a step back.

"That's everyone." Sandman walked up beside me, his eyes growing wider when he saw the woman. "Calla? Are you okay? Where are the rest of the mates?"

"I'm fine, Sandman." Calla turned his way after giving me one last, hard look. "I haven't seen the girls, though. They left for the campground a while ago. Jameson thinks they may be in the other safe room."

I caught Sandman's eye, seeing the worry there, hoping Calla missed it. But by the way she glared at me, I knew she hadn't.

"I'm sure that's it," Sandman said, his voice a fake c: "We'll check on them. Go make yourself and baby Ali comfortable, okay? This will all be over soon."

"Fine." She turned to walk farther into the safe room but stopped and spun before I could close the door, clutching that little bundle against her chest. "If you see Beast, make sure you tell him we're safe. He'll be crazy worried if he can't find me and Ali. I don't want him distracted because of us."

"Absolutely. I'll make sure he knows," Sandman replied.

I closed the door and engaged the lock before she could say anything else, knowing we needed to act quickly. Still, my chest twinged with an odd pang of guilt for lying to her...and getting called out on it. Sandman must have felt the same way because he looked as if he'd killed someone's kitten.

"They're not in the other safe room," he said.

I sighed. "I know."

"So what do we do?"

"Fuck me." I ran a hand through my hair and sighed. "I don't even think the Detroit guys are in town yet, so they have no clue what's going on. Those bastards outside haven't moved since they tried to blow out the front of the house, and no one's going to be willing to make a move until we know the situation."

"Most of the guys upstairs" —Sandman huffed and ran a hand down his face, exhaustion showing— "they're primarily Borzohn shifters. They're not going to be willing to risk anything for a couple of witches, no matter who they're mated to. They'll go for the humans, but Zuri, Scarlett, and Amber will be on their own."

"Yeah, I figured that as well." Growling, tension in my back growing, I shook my head. "Fuck, Sandman. It's got to be on us. We need to get to the campground right away."

"There's no way off the property without going through that

said as he walked up, a noticeable limp
shifter, but I didn't recognize him. What
his expression. He was a man wearing a
ge fueled by what could only be fear. "We're
nd they're stuck out there all alone."
he hell are you?" I growled.

"Hold u, Sandman said, putting a hand on my chest to stop my advance. "This is Rex, son of Alpha Wariksen from the Valkoisus pack and brother to the Gatekeeper's mate, Kaija."

"And mate to a woman who went to the campground to help the rest of the women make sure things were ready." Rex ran a hand through his hair and released a growl. "She's human, and she's small. She's the least aggressive person I've ever met in my life. You might as well offer up a bunny rabbit to these guys. I have to get to her."

Sandman shook his head. "But if the grounds are surrounded—"

"The tunnels," I interrupted, turning for the spot Bez had pointed out on the map less than an hour before. "There are tunnels leading under the cemetery to the river. The camp where the carnival is set up is on the same river, just a bit farther south. The tunnels may be a way to sneak out."

Their bootsteps echoed along with mine as we jogged deeper into the basement. Not too far past my room, neatly hidden in a dark alcove off the main hall, we came to a large, steel porthole cover, the kind used on ships or submarines.

"What do you think we should do?" Sandman asked. Before I could answer, Rex jumped in front of the two of us, grabbing the round handle and growling as he forced it to turn. Within seconds, the airlock popped and the door swung open, revealing a dark passageway. The scent of decay filled the space, the damp earth slick in the low light leaking past the doorway.

I shrugged and nodded my head toward the tunnel. "I think we should get our asses into that tunnel if we want to make sure these women survive the day."

"What about Bez?"

"There's no time. We can't be—" I snarled, a deluge of memories swamping me, of heat and metal buildings and the acrid scent of blood as I opened a door, slowly, not rushing "—fuck, we can't be late. They need us now, and we run the risk of losing them with every minute that passes."

"Okay," Sandman said, chin up, warrior face firmly in place. "Then we go without backup."

"Yup, so get your ass in the tunnel."

He balked and shook his head. "No way. Age before beauty."

"You're older than me."

"If you ladies are afraid of the dark, I'll help you out." Rex shoved past us and led the way through the damp space, setting a solid pace just under a jog, limp and all. I followed, my eyes not adjusting to the gloom as much as I would have liked.

"Fuck," Rex exclaimed when I stepped on his heel for the third time. "Watch where you're going."

"Dude, even with my wolf eyes, I can't watch where I'm going." I slowed a bit, trying to track his steps but finding it next to impossible with the weird echo of the space. "This place is like some kind of funhouse shit gone wrong. It's darker than sin down here."

Sandman huffed from right behind me. "Make some noise."

I looked in his direction, only seeing black. "What?"

"Not you, Jameson. Rex. We'll know where you are if you make some noise. Our ears will pinpoint you."

"Oh," Rex said, still jogging. "What kind of noise?"

"Fuck me," I hissed as he splattered mud up my pant leg. At least I hoped it was mud. "Just talk, will ya?"

"It's a lot of pressure to fill silence that way. My mind is blanking."

"How'd you meet her?" Sandman asked.

"Who? Lanie?" Rex's voice rebounded in the space as we

followed a curve, sounding slightly winded.

"If that's your mate, yeah." Sandman bumped into me, cursing an apology under his breath as the floor began to angle up.

"Her boyfriend's car broke down on a road by pack land."

"Boyfriend?" I shook my head and grinned, even though he couldn't see me. I'd seen a handful of matings in my time where one of the pair was in a relationship when fate intervened. They never seemed to go well…especially not for the nonmated partner.

"Yeah," Rex growled. "The fucker was a right bastard, too. It took me months to convince her to dump him, then even more time to get her to trust me. All the while she was with him, he was smacking her around, and I had no idea."

I growled low and deep, remembering a sunny smile in the desert light that I'd never had a chance to see. "I hope you killed the fucker."

"I did, but only after he almost killed her. She couldn't see how dangerous he was for a long fucking time." Rex's voice grew softer as he said, "We fought like hell to find our happiness, and I haven't had nearly enough time with her yet. I don't know if I can survive without her."

A smile in the sun, tears in the shower, blank green eyes staring across an expanse of concrete.

"You can." My voice came out on a quiet growl, my gut turning even as my heart went out to the guy. "It sucks ass and you never forget, but you can survive…if you want to."

I shook my head, the warmth of the tunnel along with the comfort of the soothing blanket of darkness around us making me soft. Weak. Open.

"Sandman did," I said, my voice barely above a whisper. "And I did, too."

Silence can be a weighty thing at times. Dark and oppressive. Tense in a way that spoke of danger and pain. The silence in that tunnel turned all of those in a split second.

"You lost your mate?" Rex finally asked.

I swallowed hard, glad for the lack of light so the two men wouldn't see how much this hurt to talk about. "Yeah, last year."

"I'm really sorry, man. How long were you together?"

"We weren't."

"Huh?" He stumbled, the sound of his stuttering footsteps bouncing around the small space.

"We weren't together...we'd never met." I took a deep breath, the memories of that day making my head hurt and my stomach sour. "I was on a job for the Feral Breed, hunting down some small-time group of thugs who'd broken in to our denhouse in Flagstaff and smashed some shit. I found out where their headquarters were and had gone to beat some sense into the fuckers, but I was too late. The warehouse they'd set up in was filled with bodies, some dead, some almost. A vamp had taken them out."

I closed my eyes for a moment, slowing my pace. Fuck, the memories killed me. Dead bodies had littered the ground, blood splatter on every surface. The space awash in bits and pieces of human flesh. The entire place had reeked of rot and death and blood. And my mate, my beautiful, dark, fairy-like mate, had been smack in the center of it all.

"I'd been too late to save her. She was already gone."

"Jesus," Rex hissed. "How'd you know she was your mate?"

It took me a second to find my answer, too lost in the memory of that day. "Her eyes were open, blank in death, but staring toward the door." *Green eyes...wide eyes...eyes that brightened when she smiled...went smoky when I teased her with my fingers. Eyes that stared into mine every time we made love slowly in the morning light.* "As soon as I saw her, I knew. I felt the pull. But then the sense of mate disappeared, and I was left with nothing but the scent of her death."

"I'm really sorry, man." Rex huffed a breath, almost

groaning in what sounded like pain…the physical kind. This trek couldn't have been easy on him.

"Yeah, well…fate isn't always in your favor, you know?" I shook off the melancholy, digging deep for some anger instead. "That's my sob story. We'll get your Lanie back so you don't have one of your own to tell."

Those words tasted false, hard to achieve, but I hoped. Hell, I might have even prayed a bit.

"And you lost your mate as well, Sandman?" Rex asked.

"Yeah," Sandman said. "Pack dispute."

"That explains why you were so adamant about Gates and my sister not staying with us."

I snorted. "Gates will never leave the Feral Breed. The man was made for the life."

"Apparently, so was my sister. I thought about joining for all of five seconds, but then some fucker shot me in the knee."

"That why you limp?" I asked.

"Yeah, there's no way that was going to heal right. But hey, I got an honorary road name from Bez out of the deal."

I tripped, barely catching myself before hitting the muddy floor. That wasn't anything I'd expected to hear. "What's that?"

"After the fight, he named me Cappers. Said it was for jumping in to save my sister because—"

"She's an Omega," I finished for him.

"Exactly."

"That's a huge deal. You understand that, right?" And it was. Bez didn't bestow any kind of respect lightly. He and his Cleaners were hard as ice, their only soft spot being the Omegas, the female shifters with the power to strengthen pack bonds. The same women someone had been kidnapping and we'd been hunting.

"I know," Rex said. "He and I had a little talk after I was shot. It was enlightening, both about the naming honor and shifter life in general. He helped me bring a lot of harmony back to my pack. We're stronger than ever now."

"I don't trust packs." Sandman's voice was hard and cold, brittle in the deep silence. Not that I blamed him. If I'd been in his shoes, I'd be just as distrustful as he was. He'd been a good pack wolf, happy even, but his Alpha had called Prerogative on his mate. That barbaric custom—a pack Alpha being able to basically rape any woman in his pack at his whim—was something I could never understand, let alone stand for. Neither could Sandman, so he'd challenged his Alpha to keep his mate safe. Sadly, the Alpha female had snuck in while Sandman was fighting and killed his mate herself, the jealous bitch cutting through protocol and acting out of turn. She'd paid for her arrogance, but that meant little to Sandman. His mate was still dead.

"We're not that way, you know," Rex said, making Sandman and me both growl.

"Not now." Sandman's tone ended the conversation, but my thoughts were stuck. Dishonest leaders and men without morals. Pack politics and dangerous secrets. The heat of the desert afternoon, the steel building baking in the sun, the stench of death. Dead mates, no matter what the situation.

The scent of *her* death was one I'd never forget…the pain one I didn't know if I could live through much longer. I had no idea how Sandman had lasted as long as he had since his mate was killed.

Light infiltrated the tunnel as the floor angled up sharply, leading us to the surface. The change in topography was enough to make my mind focus back in on the problem at hand… saving Rex's Lanie and the other women at the campground. Sandman and I had both failed with our own mates—we couldn't fail again.

We came to a concrete shelf with a round opening to the outside. Rex hopped up first, ducking through to exit the tunnel. I followed behind him, my shoulders scraping the sides of the walls on the way out. Cool, clean air quickly replaced the stink of rot. Clean air and the scent of shifters nearby.

"Where to?" Rex asked as he reached the end of the concrete hole, dropping down to the riverbank. I followed then looked back where we'd been, memorizing the way home in case we actually succeeded in getting the women to safety. The entrance to the tunnel was hidden in the design of a small concrete bridge that supported the road above. Shallow circles carved into the concrete added depth to what was basically a stone wall. Most were merely there for decoration, but the circle leading to Merriweather was deeper, not that you could easily tell. Hidden under the support bracings of the bridge above, almost invisible to the naked eye, the tunnel entrance stood in shadow, the depth of the circle concealed by the design of the bridge itself. Ingenious, really—hiding in plain sight.

"The camp is south," Sandman said, ducking as he crawled out of the tunnel. "We'll need to cross to the other bank at some point, but that might be better to do once we pass the dam."

"Good idea," I said and took off at a jog heading south. We followed the bank of the river, staying hidden within the tree line to avoid the possibility of being seen. The area was pretty remote, but that didn't mean there weren't humans about or scouts from the group surrounding the Fields. We needed to be invisible for as long as possible if this plan was going to work.

The terrain remained relatively flat and smooth, the trek taking almost no time at all, which was good for Rex. His limp had gotten worse, but his face was set. That man wouldn't have stopped or slowed down for anything, not with his mate in danger. I could see why Bez had bestowed an honorary road name on him—Rex had a strength of will to be respected. He would have made a powerful Feral Breed member had he not been injured. Honestly, he probably still would.

As we followed a slight easterly curve across from the north edge of the camp, the scent of shifter grew stronger. My wolf growled low, anxious, sensing how outnumbered we were.

"There," Sandman whispered, pointing. Across the bank, a line of maybe a dozen shifters a hundred yards down were approaching what looked like a tornado but wet and…covered with flames.

"What the hell is that?" Rex hissed.

I cursed low and under my breath. He was a Borzohn, a traditional pack wolf, which meant I already knew how he was going to feel about what *that* was. "My guess? The witches are using their magic to defend themselves from their attackers."

Rex's eyes went wide. "There are witches here?"

The tone of his voice said more than his words—he wasn't happy that his mate was anywhere near witches. No shifter would be, not when our instincts flared the way they did around their kind. Fear and distrust of witches was hardwired into our brains. There was nothing we could do to stop the reaction that I knew of. I had no idea how Phoenix and Shadow handled it, though they were Anbizen. Maybe changed wolves didn't have the same reaction.

Sandman pushed past us, heading for the riverbank. "Yeah, there are witches over there. And they're mated to a couple of the guys in the Feral Breed Detroit den. They're also nice women who are probably keeping the humans with them alive right now, so I'd suggest you check your disgust."

I stared after him, my eyes wide and my mouth closed. Guess some Borzohns *had* figured out how to get past their instinctive response to witches. Sandman surprised me, and that wasn't easy to do.

"Fuck me," Rex said when he followed Sandman down the bank, worry in his eyes. "Witches can't be trusted."

"And packs can?" Sandman spat. I held my tongue— Sandman had Rex there. The younger wolf didn't answer, simply stepped into the water to follow Sandman across. I stayed at the back, keeping an eye on Rex just in case. That leg wasn't going to hold up to much more abuse, and we hadn't even reached the fight yet.

We swam across the river slowly, staying quiet, keeping our eyes southward. We couldn't see the front line, but the shifters making up the rear of the assault team crept toward where we assumed the witches stood at the base of the whirlwind, completely oblivious to our approach. Which was a good thing. There were more wolves than the three of us could handle, and I wasn't sure what those witches were capable of. The carnies, at least, appeared to have headed for the hills, as I couldn't sense anyone else around. That crew was smart, though they'd been around shifters, vamps, and all manner of humans with powers for decades. They knew the ropes.

Once we reached the opposite bank, we crept behind the line of shifters, still in our human forms. We'd need to shift before our attack, but not yet. Not until we'd gotten closer. Once we could blend in to what I hoped was a group of shifters thrown together at the last minute and not a true team. That would give us a few seconds to hide within their ranks before we started cutting them down. Our only chance to win against a group that large was to surprise the enemy.

Before we could reach the wolves, though, the scream of a powerful engine revving hard broke the relative quiet. I dropped into a crouch, snarling and ready to attack. Bright orange sparks shot into the air over the bridge just south of the witches. Metal on concrete screeched a tremendous off-key song as a motorcycle went flying over the railing of the bridge and headed for the water below. A very custom, completely unique World War II XA motorcycle, to be exact. One I'd ridden next to on numerous missions over the past year.

A tiger, huge and snarling, jumped over the fence at the south end of the property and raced toward the waterspout. At first, I stared, unable to believe my eyes, but then the cogs began to work together. I'd always known Shadow kept some kind of secret, the whispers about him being a mutt something I caught occasionally but never really listened to or believed. But to see him—to actually see a tiger and know he was the man I'd been working with all this time—still struck me stupid. The purists in the NALB were going to have a field day trying to fry his ass if they found out. And I was going to make sure I stood beside him and chewed each of their asses out in his defense. My partner had proven himself time and again. Hybrid or pure wolf, he was still Shadow, one of the best of our breed.

Two wolves followed Shadow into the campground, both having to take the longer way around the fence since they didn't have the strength to go over it. As they headed for the base of the spout, I easily recognized the lead one as Rebel in his wolf form. The second I could only assume had to be Phoenix, coming to rescue his mate along with the other guys.

Well, fuck me running, Feral Breed Detroit to the rescue.

"Looks like the cavalry's here," Sandman whispered. "But where the hell did the kitty cat come from?"

"That tiger was the one riding the bike that went over the edge," I said. "Which means our friend Shadow has a secret up his ruff."

"Holy shit, that's a hell of a secret." Rex stared as the giant cat dove right through the wall of wind, water, and flames.

"Good thing he's a hell of a good man." I pulled a knife from my pocket, flipping the blade open with a flourish. "I'm going to assume his new mate, one of those witches we already talked about, is in that spout and needs our help just as much as your Lanie. Keep that in mind when you see those stripes."

Rex glared, his chin up in a subtle challenge. "I remember Shadow—he fought for my sister when those fuckers took her. Those stripes are nothing but window dressing to me."

I smirked, liking this kid more and more. "Good. Now, let's go save a few mates. Lead the way, Rex; we've got your back."

I rushed forward the second Rex took off running, staying in my human form as wolves jumped and snarled around me. Rex raced directly for the base of the waterspout where I assumed his mate had to be, so I followed him into the fray. Backing him up. Making sure he reached Lanie. Just because Sandman and I had lost our mates didn't mean Rex had to suffer the same fate. Someone deserved a happily ever after, for fuck's sake.

As Rex made it inside the spout with the rest of the mated couples, the magic burst—the energy dissipating—and the wall of wind, fire, and water disappeared. The attacking wolves surged forward, ready to take out the witches. I focused on eliminating the fuckers from the back of the pack, knowing Sandman was already working in his human form from the front toward me. One by one, I sliced through wolf necks, slowly making my way across the field. Waves of water crashed over us, and fireballs occasionally went screaming past, but still we fought. I could only hope those witches knew who the good guys were in this battle.

As I grabbed a particularly large wolf and pulled him to my chest, he twisted and slashed at my forearm, making me drop my knife. Growling, I yanked him against me, hands on either side of his head to break his neck. Before I could, though, a van raced up the road at the edge of the camp, squealing to a stop right in front of the campground entrance. Gates, Kaija, and Klutch jumped out the side door, immediately shifting to their wolf forms and running to join the fight. Relief flooded me. Gates and Klutch were good fighters, and Kaija was an Omega. Her power would feed our strength. The odds had definitely turned in our favor.

I cracked the wolf's neck and dropped him, grabbing my knife to slit his throat. But a flicker in my periphery caught my attention. Made me look up. Two more people ran from the van, too small to be wolf shifters. One male raced around the front and down the hill, bland and inconsequential as he ran through the gates. The other, a female, hopped out of the passenger seat and immediately snared every bit of my attention. Small, dark, fairy-like…she stirred something inside of me. Something I'd thought was gone. Something that made a flare of pain sear through my bones and solidify in my chest.

And when her green eyes found mine, I swear my heart stopped beating.

"Not possible…" The words floated around me even though I didn't know if I'd actually said them. There was no way… She'd died. I'd seen her blank eyes, smelled her death all over that goddamned warehouse. And yet, standing on the other side of the fence a mere fifty yards away was the woman I'd seen in my mind for the past year. The root of all my pain and grief, the source of all my sexual fantasies. My mate.

"What the…" I dropped the incapacitated wolf, taking two steps toward the woman. She watched me, smiling soft and kind, exactly like the picture in my head. So much so that I thought I would die from the joy. But then her eyes grew wide, and fear took over her face. Scared, my mate was scared. I snarled, ready to run to her, to protect her. To do whatever it took to banish that look from her face forever.

She shouted something I couldn't hear, stepping toward me, something in her hand and pointed my way. At the same time, a heavy weight slammed into my back, knocking me to my knees. A wolf attacked, snarling and biting, having taken advantage of my distraction. I rolled, protecting my stomach and neck, but I was at a severe disadvantage. There was no way I could shift with him on top of me, and my human form was no match for his wolf one. If he nicked an artery and I bled out, that would be the end for me, and I'd just seen a reason to live a little longer.

Luckily, I hadn't dropped my knife.

I pushed and slashed, trying to keep my eyes on my opponent but finding myself more concerned with her. With my mate. Where was she? What was she doing here? Was she safe? I needed to get this fucker off me and find her. Protect her. I couldn't go through the pain of the last year again, couldn't lose her after nothing more than a glance.

As I roared and stabbed my blade into the wolf's neck, an arrow came flying through the air, landing in the wolf's chest with a thunk. The beast faltered, stumbling back as his eyes rolled and his tongue lolled out of his mouth. Before I could stand up, she was there, standing over me. A huntress with her bow. Her long, dark hair wild and whipping in the wind, her face set in a scowl as she looked out across the remaining wolves circling us. And yet she didn't falter. She planted her feet on either side of me and raised her bow, aiming into the crowd of wolves, drawing the string to her cheek. Ready to fight.

FOUR

Aoife

MY HEART RACED AS I guarded the fallen man, the one who'd haunted me, who I'd secretly been searching for. The one I had never expected to find. But I had found him, though I didn't know if I wanted to wrap my arms around him or punch him. For a year—a full damned year!—he'd tortured me. Invading my dreams, pictures of his eyes popping into my head at the worst times, sinfully delicious visions of the two of us together teasing me, making me crazy with lust. Making me swear off other men since there was no way they could compete with him. I'd seen that man naked more times than I could count, had memories of doing things with him I'd never done but really, really wanted to, and yet this was the first time we'd ever been so close. The first time I knew he was real.

It wasn't just the sex dreams that had kept me yearning for him. There were sweet moments that felt too real to disregard, as well. The way he smiled at me when he caught me zoning out, how he'd touch the side of my face or kiss my palm in a quiet moment. The simple feel of his arms wrapped around me in the middle of the night. He'd been my friend, my source of affection, and my lover for a year… in my head. And suddenly there he was, on the ground at my feet. Staring up at me with the widest, bluest eyes I'd ever seen. In a ridiculously precarious position, flat on his ass with nothing to defend himself but a knife.

Stupid men.

Keeping him in my peripheral vision but doing my best to ignore him at the same time, I continued my assault on the attacking wolves. Releasing my arrows when the shot presented itself, aiming for their hearts, giving the others who'd driven with Percy and me a chance to take down as many attackers as they could. Percy stayed close by me, half guarding, half watching the future to direct my shots.

Wolf after wolf fell, both to my arrows and to the others who I assumed were all on the good side. I saw the big, black wolf fighting with the smaller white—those two were obvious. The rest seemed to range from tan to dark gray, too alike for me to be able to tell them apart. A huge, light-colored wolf near the riverbank fought loudly, his snarls and barks distracting. A woman with an obvious baby bump stood close behind him, controlling what looked like a ten-foot-tall wave of water moving across the grass. She had to be one of the witches the coven had brought up, the Weavers. Strong and focused, she was some kind of pregnant powerhouse. I liked her on sight.

Another couple fought nearby, a woman throwing balls of flames at enemy wolves as her tiger—holy shit, an actual *tiger*—sliced his way through anyone who tried to get close to her. The two fought viciously, no sign of weakness in their attack. And they fought together, completely in sync as a team. In fact, most of these wolves seemed to be paired up, at least the ones I assumed were on the good side of the line, which made my job a little easier. I'd ignore the pairs and go for the lone wolves, hoping not to make a mistake. I didn't want to shoot an ally, but I also didn't want to risk letting an enemy slip through the line and go for one of the non-wolves.

Eventually—which was really probably only a few seconds but seemed so much longer—the man on the ground rose to his feet behind me. He stayed close, though, backing me up with his knife. I could feel him, hear his breaths, and see the motions of his arms as he fought just out of my line of sight. I wanted to turn and watch him, wanted to stare, but I needed to focus. We had the enemy line broken—it wouldn't take long to destroy them with the way we were all fighting together. Already, the majority of the attacking wolves were down. Just a few more, and we'd win.

The fighting paused as an explosion sounded. We spun as a unit, turning to see what had happened. A carousel burned along the driveway into the campground, smoke billowing from the top, parts and pieces scattered all over the grass. I saw the distraction for what it was—the attackers' last chance at breaking through our concentrated defense and gaining the upper hand. Their plan failed, though. Instead of losing focus, we tightened up our defensive line as if sharing the same thoughts. We moved into a knot in the center of the field, forming a circle around two women who weren't fighting, facing the last of our attackers head on. A wall of strength and bravery protecting what I assumed were the weakest links—the humans.

Faced with a line of six wolves, two men who'd fought as warriors, three witches, a tiger, and me, the survivors wisely chose to race off into the woods. A cowardly act, but one I understood perhaps better than most. For all the lip service one might hear, very few people were actually willing to give their life for a cause. Not without one hell of a reason. That thought reminded me of the man I'd been dreaming about, seeing him lying on the ground in the middle of a battle, of the way I'd rushed through a sea of wolves to get to him. To protect him. In that moment, he'd been my hell of a reason. Now, he was just another stranger. Sort of.

As the last attacking wolf disappeared over the hill, the group relaxed almost as a whole…but not me. I didn't drop my arms. If I relaxed, I'd have to turn. I'd have to look at *him*, the one who'd consumed my thoughts for so long. The one I felt so connected to. The man who both attracted me and scared the shit out of me. The man I didn't know.

"You know, next time Blaze wants to throw a party, I'm RSVP'ing with a negative." A dark-haired woman with bright pink burns running up and down her arms stepped away from the circle, the tiger following close behind her. "I think I'd rather stay home and play with my pussy than deal with this shit."

"Scarlett," another woman said, her arms crossed and an exasperated look on her face.

"What?" She tried to pull off big, innocent eyes, but there was a glint in them that said too much about where her mind was. She grabbed the tiger around the muzzle and brought his face up to hers, pushing their cheeks together as he grumbled a sound that was not quite a growl. "Look at this pretty pussy? Can you blame me for wanting to play with him?"

"Pretty sure he's going to bite your ass if you call him a pussy again, Scarlett," a blond man interjected. A very naked blond man with a woman wrapped tightly in his arms. What was with these people and their lack of clothes?

She grinned. "Yeah, Rebel. He might. But I like it."

"Lovely. You want to work your magic on these bodies so we can call this job complete?"

The tiger growled, a violent, terrifying sound. Scarlett placed her injured hand on his head, petting him. Calming him.

"Sure. No problem."

As the circle broke into smaller groups and conversations began in earnest, strong arms wrapped around me. Ones I'd known most of my life and yet felt wrong since they weren't the ones I wanted holding me up. Percy pressed himself against my side and forced my bow down. I took a deep breath, releasing it as my arms dropped. No more hiding, no avoidance. This was it.

"You ready?" Percy asked, his eyes on mine, his hands gripping my biceps and keeping me from trembling.

Before I could answer, my dream man growled like an animal. Like a wolf. I spun, staring, taking him in fully for the first time. And *oh my*, the visions hadn't done him justice. He was bigger, stronger, and rougher than I'd expected, with a long body covered in curve after curve of muscle, accentuated by his wet jeans and T-shirt. But the look on his ridiculously handsome face turned my stomach. He glared at Percy as if my best friend were some kind of threat, as if he had some kind of claim on me. As if his opinion of who should or should not be touching me mattered. That thought threw me right past being afraid of what was next and straight into fuck-no mode. No one told me what to do.

"You can drop that pissed-off expression right now, mister." I glared as the man looked at me, all gorgeous and irate, eyes going wide at my tone. "Without Percy by my side, you'd still be flat on your ass, and we all might be dead."

His growl immediately cut off and his face crumpled. The urge to run to him, to soothe that pain, was fierce, something I hadn't expected. But I resisted. Even though I felt a draw between us, had spent a year avoiding most of my real life to spend my time with him in my head, I didn't *know* him. I'd seen him once for a matter of seconds, and then he'd run. Yes, he'd been in my thoughts for a year—charming me, driving me wild with his imagined touch, owning my heart with his smile— but that wasn't real. Those were dreams and fantasies. The man standing before me *was* real, and no matter how grateful I was to see him in the flesh, he was pissing me off.

When I didn't back down, he looked away. And then he

took off. The sting of it, of him dismissing me without a word, cut deep. It left me unsure of what to do next, how to talk to him. If I even wanted to.

"We have to get back to the Fields," he hollered over his shoulder, his back to me as he headed for the riverbank. "They're surrounded and could be in a full-out war as we speak. They need our help."

My stomach sank. So this was it? We drove all this way, chased the connection between him and me, only to be dismissed? That sting grew, becoming a throbbing pain in my heart.

"What about the carnies?" I asked, desperate to delay the inevitable. "I can't imagine you want people to know about—" I waved a hand, not sure how to describe their animal-human body cohabitation "—all that."

The man turned, his face flat, no emotion showing. "The carnies are friends of ours. They'll keep our secrets."

Percy huffed. "Some friends. I didn't see them coming to defend you."

Dream man dropped the calm, glaring once more. "They have their own shit to worry about, including making sure humans don't find out all they can do. Don't make them out to be cowards when they were simply protecting their interests."

I swallowed hard and turned away, almost embarrassed by how his gritty voice turned me on. This whole day had gotten so weird and been so long. I just wanted to head back to the van and get on the road. Maybe cry a little bit at the loss of a man I'd never had in the first place. Maybe break a few things instead.

"We're going to have to cross the river," one man said, a blond who'd stayed human during the fight like my...not my...like *him*. "Wolves, go wolf. Everyone else can pair up with a wolf to help make it across."

One man with white-blond hair like Kaija wrapped his

arms around a brunette woman, obviously trying to soothe her. "You'll be fine, Lanie. Just hang on to me, and I'll get you across."

"I hate the water," she whispered.

"I know, but this isn't Lake Superior and I'll be right beside you." He kissed her head and smiled down at her. "At least the water's not cold enough to shrivel my junk again. Last time was downright embarrassing."

Lanie giggled, still looking nervous. "I barely noticed."

"You were staring. Don't lie."

"You were naked. I couldn't help myself."

"Thank the gods for that."

The connection between the two made me ache, made my heart stir for something I'd never experienced. They truly cared about each other; they had history together. The only person I had history with was Percy. Not that I didn't love him like family, but something more might be a little…nice. Not that I'd find it here.

"You got your mate, Rex?" my dream man asked, lifting his chin toward the adorable couple I'd been watching.

"Absolutely, Jameson. And I'm not letting her go again."

Jameson. His name was Jameson. Why did such a simple thing make my heart go all fluttery?

Jameson's blue eyes met mine, hard and intense, looking almost pissed off as he took me in. "Smart man."

"Can you swim?" a woman asked, directing her question at me. Jade green eyes met mine, and a small dimple appeared when she smiled. Beautiful was the only way to describe her.

But her smile faltered and her eyes went unfocused just as Percy gasped.

"You're Amber," Percy said.

"Amber Weaver." The woman nodded once but frowned, her brow furrowing. "Do I know you?"

"Not yet, sweetheart, but we're going to be besties real soon.

The name's Percy, and I'm a precog like you."

Her face fell, paling. "It's…nice to meet you, Percy."

Percy watched her, his head tilted. "What are you—"

"Everyone ready?" the clothed blond man interrupted, giving Amber the opportunity to walk away. "It's time to take a swim,"

"I don't swim," I said, taking a step back. "But we have a van over there."

He cocked his head in a way that wasn't quite human. "You won't make it to the mansion in a car—they have the place surrounded. You're going to have to come through the tunnel with us."

"Oh," I whispered, not sure if I should be happy or pissed at this development. My time with Jameson wasn't over just yet. My eyes flitted to him, unable to resist the draw to the man who'd been haunting my dreams for a year. He watched me, his face harsh again, making my chest tighten. Making my temper flare.

"Fine." I tossed my hair and looked to Percy, who seemed lost in a vision as he stared after Amber and, therefore, no help to me. "But I need to grab some of my arrows out of the van first. I don't want to be left without anything to fight with. And I don't swim."

Don't swim was an understatement. Other than pools, I'd avoided any water like the plague for over a decade. Most people would if they had my gift. Unsettled spirits tended to stick to where they passed, and people drowned all the time. No thanks.

"I'll grab the arrows," Gates said, surprising me, rushing with Kaija back to the van.

"I'll help you across the river," the clothed blond man said, reaching for my hand. Jameson growled again, deeper this time. The stranger whipped his head in Jameson's direction, the rest of his body freezing as if waiting for an attack.

"I can make sure she gets across," Percy said, pulling me away from the two men. Jameson didn't say a word. He scowled and turned his back on us, continuing toward the river. Percy gave me a look filled with secrets, an evil glimmer in his eyes. "This is going to be fun."

"What do you know?" I asked, following him to the water's edge.

"Almost everything, remember? But apparently not as much as the beautiful Amber. I'm going to be tracking her down when we get to where we're going." His eyes went unfocused as he stared down the river. Looking. Searching for something. Shaking his head once he had. "You'll be fine; they won't bother you too much. Now hush and get ready to get wet."

Wolves entered the water first, many carrying those weird cloaks in their mouths, swimming in pairs. Each human—or witch, I supposed—was escorted across the river by a wolf except for Scarlett. Her tiger swam beside her, his orange stripes practically glowing in the dull brown water. Gates and Kaija swam in human form, carrying boxes of arrows across for me. Everyone made it to the opposite bank just fine, but when it came time for Percy and me, I balked.

"I don't think I can."

Jameson gripped my elbow, surprising me, his touch demanding my attention. He stood silent, still and staring. Deep, sky-blue eyes entranced me, dragged me under their spell. Made me feel wanted in ways I'd never known.

"I'm with you," he said, his voice low and soft. I shivered as the sound washed over me. His eyes, his voice, his skin on mine—all familiar and yet not. I'd felt his touch every day for months, kissed those lips a thousand times, but this was the first time we'd met. Everything between us, every memory I had, was a lie. He had no idea who I was.

I didn't know why fantasies of us together had bombarded me for the past year, or what the pull was that brought me to him, but it didn't matter. I was here now, in danger and heading for a war I had no real want to fight. I'd have to suffer through being near Jameson without being *with* him until Percy and I could leave.

I finally nodded, surrendering to the fact that all my dreams were lies. He gripped me tighter for a moment, his hand hot and strong. My skin tingled, my body craving more of his touch. I opened my mouth to say something to him, not that I had any idea what, but he released me and shifted to his wolf form without saying a word, walking into the water without a glance back.

And again, that dismissal stung in a way I wished it hadn't.

Percy and I entered the water together, him holding my backpack as I lofted my bow above the waterline. When the river grew too deep to stand, Percy swam a backstroke, keeping his eyes on me the entire way. The wolf stayed right beside me as well, close enough to touch if I wanted to. Not that I did. Actually touch, that is… I sure as hell wanted to.

Spirits chilled me as I swam, dismembered voices rising up through the water. I ignored them and kept swimming. They were too far away, too soft to do much more than give me a headache. Something I was utterly grateful for.

When the three of us reached the opposite bank, Jameson's wolf shook off the water and bounded after his teammates, leaving Percy and me alone. Again.

"This is so weird," I whispered, holding my bow between my knees so I could wring out my hair.

"This is nothing. Once we get to this Merriweather place…" He trailed off, shaking his head. "Stay close to him, okay?"

"Who?"

"Jameson. I'm not kidding about tracking down this Amber witch. I think I'm going to be busy."

"He doesn't want me around him."

"You're wrong," Percy said, his voice sure and forceful. I

doubted, though. I doubted hard. "Just be open to spending time with him. The rest will all work out if you are."

"Whatever," I said with a sigh, too tired to wish, too afraid to give in to the hope his words made me feel.

We followed the wolves south until we reached the base of a bridge. Along the concrete wall that formed the supports were circles cut out, probably to be decorative. But one was more than just for looks. As Percy and I watched, Rex and his mate ducked inside, disappearing into the darkness.

"Off to the land of the hobbits," Percy whispered.

I nodded, dreading walking into that tunnel. A sense of death emanated from it, making my skin go cold. The last thing I needed was to go all necro in a group of strangers, but there was nothing else to do.

"You'll be fine," Percy whispered, holding my hand and letting the rest of the group go first. Finally, he pushed me forward with a head nod. "I'm seeing these wolfies a little better now. Trust me."

"Maybe I don't want to trust you right now."

"Too bad. Move your ass."

I sighed and crouched through the hole, grumbling about best friends and graves. But as I dropped to the ground from the concrete shelf, the mumbling stopped. The first thing that struck me was how dark and damp the space became as I walked down the sloping floor. The second was the energy of past lives coming from somewhere ahead. Lots of them...too many.

"Percy?"

My voice rebounded, echoing through the tunnel, but he didn't answer. The jackass. Certain he'd never intentionally lead me into danger, I moved forward, deeper into the dark. My breaths came faster in the heavy silence. The pressure from the dead building, coming toward me, falling from the ceiling to surround me.

The first rush of icy wind brushed my shoulder when I was

probably a hundred yards in. I closed my eyes against what I knew would be there, what I knew I'd see even through the dark.

"I'm not available right now."

Staticky squealing in my ears told me more than my eyes could. This one had been dead a long time, too far removed from his corporeal form to communicate with me, but too stubborn to give up without trying. For a soul to be around that long, there had to be something important they wanted the living realm to know. Or at least important to them. My job was to listen, my gift the ability to understand and help them transition. Sometimes following them into the plane between the living and the dead to better hear them, to finally know what they needed. Sadly, this was not the time for traversing planes. I was too scared and overwrought to do much more than shake as the cold began to swirl around me, making it almost impossible to help him.

"Please," I whispered, his feedback-like screams making my ears ache. "Not now. I'll come back for you, I promise. But right now, I need to get through this passage."

More cold, more squeals, more ghosts. They wrapped themselves around me, pulling me deeper into their deathly energy, screaming at me in their own way until my head ached. I spun, racing back the way I came but I lost my balance. I stumbled into the wall of the tunnel, recoiling from the wet and the dirt as I almost fell to my knees.

But then a hand grabbed my arm, a warm one, the same hand that had grabbed my arm before I stepped into the water. The same hand I'd felt touch me, tease me, bring me pleasure for the last year, at least in my mind. Jameson's hand.

"What's happening?" His voice broke through the squeals, held them back, and gave me a moment of peace, something that had never happened to me before.

"The dead," I whispered as the sound swelled once more

and the cold grew sharper and more dangerous. "Cold. I can't breathe. They need...and I can't."

"Fuck."

I felt his curse more than heard it as the squealing increased. My body grew colder, my heart slowing. Death came in with a chill and a slow descent into the world of the dead. A pull I had to fight to resist, one that drew me like a moth to the flame of the end. Heading to the land between was dangerous enough. Going there without preparations, without something to ground me in the living world, wasn't something I wanted to try. I didn't think I could end up stuck in that plane forever, but I wasn't willing to risk it.

Before I could fall, before I could slide right past the land of the living and into the cold reality of the place between, Jameson had his arms around me. He hoisted me to his chest, his breath caressing my face, juggling me until he held me just right. Warmth surrounded me, and the feel of his skin on mine made me cling to him. I pressed one ear against his chest, letting the sound of his heartbeat soothe me, letting it distract me from the squeals and screams. Letting his very presence keep me grounded. And then we were moving.

He ran through the tunnel as the spirits followed. They attacked from the ceiling, raining their energy all over me. Trying to reach me however they could. I fought to keep my focus on Jameson, on his heartbeat and his heat. On the way his arms rocked as he ran, how the muscles slid under his skin with each exertion.

The noises grew louder, more of them joining the cacophony. Staticky squeals of spirits mixed in with the booming voices of the newly dead, all clamoring for my attention. I whimpered, the pain in my head growing. Jameson held me tighter, his arms strong against my body. He ran for what seemed like miles, through the worst storm of spiritual resonance I'd ever experienced. But as the floor seemed to slope upward, the noises began to fade. Falling off. Left behind.

I was still shaking when he finally carried me out of the dark, damp tunnel and into what seemed more like a basement. Still cold, I held on to him for longer than I needed to, too happy being in his embrace to let go. But eventually, I knew my moment of contact needed to end. I pulled away from his chest, looking at the floor, embarrassed by how much I still wanted to press myself against him. Jameson set me down, but he didn't let me go. Instead, he trailed his hands down my arms to my elbows and held tight as I regained my balance. I looked up, taking a deep breath and reining all my courage in so I could face him, ready to thank him, but I froze. For the first time, I realized he wasn't wearing any clothes. Hugely, gloriously unclothed. And obviously happy to see me.

"Holy hell, you are *really* naked." I grimaced as the words left my mouth, not meaning to say them out loud. And definitely not meaning them the way they sounded…as if I wasn't pleased to see his body. Because I was. Really, really pleased. I couldn't stop my eyes from going back *there.*

He ignored my outburst, looking down at me with nothing but concern. "I need to know you're okay before I find some clothes."

"I'm fine. I just…you're so very naked. Not that it should matter."

One side of his mouth turned up in a smile. "Our clothes don't shift with us. Does my being naked bother you?"

"No!" I exclaimed, practically ready to demand he never wear clothes again. "Naked is good, fine. Really…good. I'm sorry; I'm all over the place right now. That tunnel was… I couldn't—" I stopped and sighed, exhausted from trying to speak clearly. "They're usually not so loud, but they were really strong in there." I shook my head, remembering the volume and the level of cold. Definitely not the norm.

"Who?"

"The dead." I waited for the disbelief I'd grown accustomed to seeing since I was a child, but it never came. Instead, his face grew even more worried, more pained.

"You can see them?"

"Sort of." I shrugged, suddenly nervous. And turned on. Ridiculously turned on. So much naked. "They're not always clear. Sometimes I only hear them, or see a wisp where their spirit is, but going through the tunnel, there were way more than normal. I've never had so many separate spirits coming at me all at once."

He growled and clenched his jaw. "If I would have known... fuck."

"What? What did I do?"

"Not you," he said, slightly defeated. Definitely guilty. "This is on me. We just ran underneath one of the largest cemeteries in the state."

I felt my face go slack. "Well, no wonder."

"Exactly." He swallowed, still staring, still holding on to me. "I'm so sorry—I had no idea. I never would have made you go through that if I'd have known. I would have found another way to bring you with me."

My heart stuttered, my lips trying hard to pull up in a smile. "You would have?"

"Of course." He inched closer, just a bit, but enough for me to notice. "So, you're okay?"

I ran my hands up his arms, wanting so badly to hug him, to press myself against his warmth again. To be wrapped in him. "I think so."

He held me tighter, the look in his eyes the same one I'd seen a hundred times before in my dreams, seeming as if he felt the same way. "I was worried back there. I'm so sor—"

"She's fine," Percy said as he stepped out of the tunnel, a bright smile on his face. "Necromancers deal with the dead all the time. She just needs something warm to wrap around her and something sweet on her lips. I'm sure I can help her with those."

I stared, blinking, hearing the double entendre in his words. Jameson glowered as he backed away from me, probably hearing the same thing. But Percy either didn't care or had some kind of plan in that brain of his. He winked and grabbed my hand, pulling me away from Jameson.

"Ready, Aoife?"

I frowned, hating the way Jameson's eyes had shuttered. Had closed me off from the emotions I'd seen there only moments before.

"Thank you," I whispered, suddenly doubting the truth of what we'd just experienced.

Jameson nodded, looking a bit lost. "Go. There's a safe room down the hall where the two of you can hole up until all this passes."

"Oh, hell no, Romeo." Percy pulled me behind him, dragging me away from Jameson. "We're not here to hole up. We're here to fight. So long as my girl has her trusty bow—and me by her side—we'll be fine."

"Shit," I hissed, knowing he was purposely egging Jameson on but not having the time to worry about it considering what wasn't in my hands. "I must have dropped my bow and backpack in the tunnel."

"I'll get them," Jameson said, turning to go back into the dark space. "You need to warm up, apparently."

And then he was gone.

"What the fuck, Percy?"

"Oh, hush. I know shit, remember?" Percy glanced over his shoulder before quickening his pace. "You are one lucky bitch. I'm so going to need the details when you take a ride on his—"

"Hey!" I smacked his shoulder. "One, no details…that's weird. Two, I doubt that's going to happen. The man can hardly look at me without going all angry-face."

"Call it what you want, but I've already seen. And can I just say again, you are one *lucky* bitch."

I bit back my grin, glancing over my shoulder, wishing I could catch one last look at him even though I knew that wouldn't be possible.

"That'd be a first."

FIVE

Jameson

I STARED AT THE bow and backpack of arrows I'd tucked into a corner of my room, feeling both guilty and excited. I probably should have taken them with me, brought them to her, but I wanted some little piece of her here. In my room… in my den. I wanted this place to smell like her. Her bow did, which made my wolf happy, but the modified quiver carried a chemical-like scent. Something familiar, but I couldn't place it. I'd have to investigate the scent later, though, because I knew Bez was going to be looking for me.

Once I threw on some clothes, I followed the scent of my mate and Percy up the stairs to the main floor of the mansion, trying my hardest to ignore their quiet whispers and hand-holding once I caught up. Trying and failing miserably. It didn't help that my wolf had become completely obsessed with her. Tracking her every move, ready to challenge the little human male if need be. My human side wasn't much better. I'd spent a year seeing her, learning all of her expressions, pinpointing her emotions in every false memory—happy, sad, contemplative, aroused. I knew her better than I knew anyone else in the world. And yet, she was a stranger to me. That reality brought anxiety with it, leaving me worrying about how to proceed. Wondering if she had any fucking clue who I was.

Her giggle floated through the air. She was laughing with Percy, not with me, and that pissed me off as jealousy reared its ugly head inside me. As much as I hated the idea, I'd have to take my time wooing her away from the punk. I wanted to steal her, mark my claim, and make sure that Percy guy knew exactly whom she belonged to, but I'd seen shifters go that route. I knew being a possessive asshole would only cause her to resist our connection longer. Like Rex had with his Lanie, I'd have to be patient, make sure she knew I was here and waiting for her. All while fighting off a pack of shifters and protecting the president of the NALB.

Nothing could be simple.

Still, as much as seeing her with him ate at me and as much as the current situation was possibly the worst timing in the world to find a mate, it was still a relief just to see her alive. I didn't know how I'd been so wrong back in the desert, but obviously, I had been. She—Aoife, the boy had said, such a pretty Irish name—was very much alive. And yet, I clearly remembered the scent of her death from that day at the warehouse. It had haunted me for the past year. Hell, she still smelled of death, yet she walked the halls, living, breathing, talking, laughing.

Staring…at me.

I stood in the doorway to the foyer, watching her, tracking her every breath with my eyes. And she stared right back. Eyes alight. Mouth pink and full. I knew that expression, had seen it in my mind a thousand times. Had jacked off to it at least half that many. She desired me. Just that look, those seconds in her gaze, made my breath pick up. Made all my blood rush to my cock. My low growl was uncontrollable, completely involuntary. Totally in response to the fire in her eyes. The way her long hair brushed the side of her face as she cocked her head. The way her pale skin flushed along the neckline of her shirt.

Good goddamn, but she was beautiful.

"Where the fuck have you been?" Bez's growled question stole my attention, but not before I saw my mate take a step back from the huge shifter. I jumped forward, acting on instinct, placing myself between the two to keep my mate safe. I knew Bez would never harm her, but she didn't. And her fear wasn't something I wanted to see.

"We went to the campground to help the women make it back." I kept my eyes on his, kept my legs slightly apart. A challenger's stare and a fighter's stance.

His face hardened as he glared at me, his eyes flicking over my shoulder to glance at the newcomers before meeting mine once more. I knew he was pissed, but I also knew he wouldn't say shit about us going after the mates. In the past, yes…he would have torn my ass apart for abandoning the president and disregarding his plans. But since he'd met his own mate a few months back, he'd softened a bit in that regard. Well, as softened as a man like Bez could get.

"All safe?" he growled, glancing over my shoulder at Aoife again. I growled louder, deeper. More violently.

"Affirmative. Some are being escorted to the safe room, though a couple have decided to fight with us."

Aoife stepped to my side, Percy next to her. I twisted a bit, keeping her at the back of my arm. Guarding her.

Bez looked over my mate and her friend. Curious. But then he shook his head.

"They'll get in the way," Bez said dismissively. "The men outside sent a messenger to the door. A shifter who goes by the name the King is challenging Blaze for the presidency. As per NALB code, they've given us until tomorrow at sundown to prepare ourselves."

"If he's challenging Blaze, why'd he bring so many fighters? And what was with the bomb?"

Bez growled and cracked his neck. "This King feels as if Blaze hides behind his Cleaners and Feral Breed members, so he brought a team with him to make sure the challenge remains fair. The bomb was apparently their way of announcing themselves."

"Dramatic fuckers, aren't they?" Shadow asked as he rubbed something white and medicinal-looking onto Scarlett's burns.

I paced, keeping close to Aoife but needing motion to help me think. "So they give us thirty hours trapped in this house without access to any of our backup teams? For what?"

"The lull we're in was all part of their plan." Percy stepped forward, head high, no longer touching my mate. "They'll come back tonight instead to finish us off. First through the front again, loudly, assuming we won't see through the distraction. Then through the back, a sneak attack with their strongest soldiers. The leader will be at the rear of the group in the back as well, though he'll stay behind the line of fighting until the end. Quite cowardly, that one."

Bez glowered, unbelieving, but then Amber, the psychic witch, the one related to Shadow's mate, spoke up.

"He's right. It'll be late tonight—front, then back. They'll try to smoke us out, I think." She glanced to where her sisters stood, tucked into the sides of their clothed mates. "Everything's a bit blurry, just like the lighthouse was when we left in the winter. As if covered in smoke."

"They burned the lighthouse," Aoife added, giving the girls an apologetic look. "That's why Percy and I drove so far north. He saw a vision of your coven being burned alive, so we came to help."

The witch sisters stared, all three of them silent and pale. Shadow and Phoenix focused on their mates, both wearing matching expressions of worry. These fuckers had attacked their mates' coven, which meant the sisters could be in danger themselves. I had a feeling the guys weren't going to be leaving the sides of their mates much over the next few hours.

Amber was the first to recover, nodding to Aoife and Percy.

"They're our ex-coven, but thank you for helping them. No one deserves to burn like that."

"Not all of them," Scarlett murmured.

"Stop it," Azurine said, closing her eyes and turning her face into Phoenix's shoulder. "Just because they kicked me out doesn't mean they deserve to die."

Scarlett sighed. "I know. I'm just…rattled."

"That's one way to put it." Azurine sniffed, giving her sisters a small, weak smile. "I can't believe the house burned, though. Even Scarlett couldn't make that place go up in flames growing up."

"I did *not* burn down the fucking porch," Scarlett spat, glaring at her sister.

"At any rate," Amber interjected, looking from one sister to the other. "Burning witches is horrific, and I'm thankful our new friends here were able to protect our former coven from such a nasty fate."

She locked eyes with Percy, looking nervous. "You and I have a lot to talk about."

Percy shrugged, feigning casual. "Whenev, sister. We got time."

"So they'll set Merriweather on fire?" Bez asked, pulling us back to the issue at hand.

"Let them try to burn us," Scarlett said with a shrug, trying hard to look unaffected but clinging to Shadow's hand. "I'm not afraid of flames. If I have a little time to recharge, I can direct whatever they start to keep the fire from spreading."

"The river's not far," Azurine said, hand on her round belly, protecting her young as she stood next to Phoenix. "We can call the corners, and I can pull the water this way. It'll bathe the house before they even make their attack to keep the flames under control once they do."

"The president of the NALB needs witches to protect Merriweather Fields. Never thought I'd see the day," Cahill said, appearing in the doorway with Killian and an exhausted looking Gideon by his side. Their group had been camped out in the medical ward since we brought back Gideon's mate, Kalie, from North Dakota. Kalie was an Omega shewolf we'd rescued from the kidnappers, one who hadn't had as easy a time or as short a stay as Bez's mate, Sariel. One who would need a few more weeks of medical care before we could release her back to her pack.

"Shut up, Cahill," Shadow growled and stepped in front of Scarlett, looking ready for a fight. Couldn't blame him, really— Cahill and he had already gone a round or two while hunting for Kalie. Bad blood ran rampant between them. "We should all be thankful they're here to help. There're a lot of shifters outside ready to kill anyone in their way."

"It's a challenge," Cahill replied, looking bored. My wolf wanted to knock him down a peg or two for it. "Blaze and this King guy duke it out. What's that got to do with the rest of us?"

Scarlett snorted. "Duh, dude. It's a cleansing."

"What's a cleansing?" he asked.

Sandman growled, shaking his head. "In packs, it's sometimes called a restructuring. If the current leader is overthrown during the challenge, the shifters who stood with the winner kill those who stood with the loser. It keeps the old guard from challenging the new guard. And that's why the King brought all those men out there. He's here to clean house, which means we're all in danger."

"Agreed," I said, growling slightly as the big shifter from North Carolina glared my way. "This isn't just about Blaze. I stand with him regardless, but there are women and children here who need protecting, and there are friends here willing to help. Let's deal with the shitstorm outside before we start tearing apart our allies. Which reminds me—" I turned my back on the Southern Appalachian shifters, showing them how little they mattered in my world "—we're beyond outnumbered, even with the Merriweather guards and what Cleaners were here when those fuckers cut us off from the outside. You called an SOS, though; there have to be Alphas and Feral Breed members behind the enemy line or on their way to help."

Bez grunted. "Yeah, but they're all at the edges of the city. I don't want them to engage without us having a way to communicate and back them up. The fuckers have us split in two."

I nodded, agreeing, seeing the same problem he did but having a bit more information. "We got out and brought the mates back through the tunnel in the basement. The one you pointed out for a water evac."

Bez's eyes locked on mine, weighing, evaluating. "Bring in reinforcements through the tunnels?"

"It could work." I shivered as Aoife brushed against me, her skin hot to the touch. She must have jumped back, though, because the contact didn't last nearly as long as I would have liked.

Bez stood quiet, eyes unfocused as we all waited. "They could lead the enemy inside."

"They could. But the tunnel isn't that big and there's a solid door on our end. As long as we place guards down there, the attack would be minimal at best." I shrugged. "No matter how big their group is, ours is better trained. We just have to get all our supporters inside the house. That's why those cowards have surrounded us. They think we won't be able to get backup. They think this will be an easy kill."

Bez paced, glancing out the windows. "Let's try it. I'll put out the word. We'll need three guards in the tunnel—one on each end and one close to the river side. There needs to be another five in the hallway, just in case. I want a heads-up if those fuckers try to get in. Any one of them steps foot inside

Merriweather, and they die. Period."

"We'll guard the tunnel," Killian said, shooting a quick glance at Cahill. "We can take the river end and monitor who comes in."

"How do we know if they should be allowed in or not?" Shadow asked.

"We add a password to the outgoing message," I said. "They have to know the password to get past Killian."

"And if the enemy finds out about the password?" Cahill asked.

"Levi can guard the terminus of the tunnel," Bez said with a wicked half smile. "That fucker will take out anyone he thinks is a threat, no questions asked."

"We've got guys from both Detroit and Kalamazoo not far from the campground," Shadow said. "If we can give them a couple of minutes to get in, they can guard the hallway. They're itching for a fight."

"Make the call," Bez said, giving Shadow a nod. "Southern Appalachian pack runs the tunnel, and Feral Breed Detroit takes the hallway. No one enters Merriweather without the password."

"What's the password?" Shadow asked.

Bez smirked. "Freckles."

"We need to find Rebel," Gates said as soon as Shadow walked off to call his team, Klutch right behind him. "We lost Numbers in the fight at the lighthouse. Rebel needs to know."

"Blessings on his soul," I whispered. I hadn't known the shifter well, but I'd seen him around when I'd been hanging at the Detroit den with Shadow. Friend or not, no club should have to deal with the loss of one of their own. We saw enough death without having it hit home so unexpectedly.

"Can you come with us, Aoife?" Kaija asked, glancing from Aoife to me and back again. "I think Rebel should get to hear what Numbers said to you."

My mate nodded once, catching my eye for a brief moment. "Of course. I'm happy to talk to whomever if it could help."

She left with Kaija and Gates, the rest of the Detroit crew and their mates following them down the long hall. Before the final corner that would take her out of my sight, she turned back, glancing my way. A single look, one moment, but it made my blood pulse in my cock. It was a look of knowing, a look of needing. She felt something between us...perhaps not exactly what I did, but something.

"What the hell was that?" Rex asked, lifting his chin to indicate the direction Aoife had gone. "You were awfully obsessed with the little necromancer. Do you know her?"

I shook my head. "Not quite. But I will."

"Explain," Bez said on a growl. "I don't want unknowns walking around the mansion without supervision. She could be with the enemy."

"She's not."

"How do you know?"

"I just do." I shrugged, ignoring the tone of his voice, knowing he never trusted anyone at first meeting. "She's my mate."

The hall went silent, the men standing around me staring as if I'd suddenly grown an extra appendage.

Rex was the first to find his wits. "I thought your mate was dead."

"So did I." Sighing, I ran a hand over my face. Tired...my body and mind were too fucking tired for all the things that needed to happen.

"How could you mistake a live girl for a dead one?" Bez asked.

"No clue. I walked into that warehouse and saw her lying on the floor, eyes open and blank. I smelled her death." I frowned, my eyebrows drawing together. "I still do sometimes."

"She lives with death every day." Percy leaned against a wall looking like an angry garden gnome as he glared up at me. "She smells like death because she walks with the dead."

I growled, stalking into his space, ready to show him who mattered when it came to my mate. Arrogant little fucker. "Maybe she needs someone better to protect her."

The bastard laughed. "Protect her from what...the dead? Yeah, good luck with that."

"I sure didn't see you helping her through the tunnel."

"No, because I saw you two never quite connecting if I interrupted, so I stayed back and let you save the day." He stepped right up to me, unafraid, the little shit honestly trying to stare me down. "She saw you at that warehouse, you know."

I blinked. Blinked again as his words rattled through my head. "What?"

"That day you came to take on the Bastard Eights. She saw you through her trance. She felt the connection to you and knew her soul mate was coming...and then she lay there, helpless and alone, and watched you leave her in the middle of that carnage."

I took a step back, my blood running cold. "She was dead."

"No, she was in death's trance. That happens sometimes when there are too many spirits around her. A vamp had taken out that whole gang. Aoife went there for help from some of the members she trusted, and she barely made it out alive. She had to fight her way back from the land between the living and the dead for three solid days. Alone. That's how long it took me to track her down so I could help her. Though I guess you would have known that had you actually stopped to check on her."

An arrow, much like the ones my mate shot, pierced my heart. "No. I saw her...I smelled her. She was dead."

"Not everything is as it seems," Amber said, joining Percy, the two crowding me.

"Exactly," Percy agreed. "She wasn't dead. She was tranced

out and stuck in the land between death and life. When the dead stay on this plane, they're sometimes too hard to see and hear. She's one of the few with the ability to travel to their realm. She communicates easier with them there and can bring back that information once she rejoins our plane. But it's a struggle for her, and sometimes those bastards don't want her to leave. Selfish motherfuckers, the dead."

I paced the length of the hall, my mind stuck on the events of that day in the desert. Like a movie playing on a loop, every moment reminded me. Repeating. Crushing me in guilt. The door...the smell...the blood...the wide green eyes. The pain.

"What about the tunnel?" I finally asked, remembering how she'd stumbled. How she'd clung to me when I picked her up. "She wasn't in a trance then, was she?"

"No, that was spirits on this plane attacking her. When spirits stay here, there's usually a reason for it. Some unfinished business they feel is important. When they sense a necromancer like Aoife nearby, they tend to swarm, which is why she usually avoids cemeteries. She had no idea the tunnel led directly under one."

"Fuck." I fisted my hand in my hair and tugged. Hard.

"Yeah, but that's everyday life for her, along with crappy apartments, not being able to work because of spirits tracking her down and screaming at her, criminals using her as their pawn in some fucked-up power struggle, and an overall shit hand of luck in regards to life." He moved closer, dropping his voice. "She's seen you for a year, dreamed of you, been haunted by you, and not known why. But I have. I saw you the first time I met her when we were kids. I've been waiting for you to rescue her like some goddamned Prince Charming. But instead of taking two fucking minutes to check on her, you bailed. You ran like a little bitch and left her there to suffer."

My snarl was loud and rough, but it died quickly. He was right. If I'd only taken a moment, really investigated the warehouse, I would have known she was alive. Maybe. She certainly looked dead at the time. Which was why I'd suffered for this past year. But she wasn't dead, and I was wasting time.

"What do I do?"

"Man the fuck up, daisy." Percy smirked, the little shit.

I rolled my eyes. "That's helpful, fucker."

"Fine," Percy said as he once again stepped into my space. "You want help? Here you go. She's not with me, never has been, so cut the crap where I'm concerned. You'll only piss her off. Don't play games, don't dillydally, and don't hold back because you think she needs to come to you. She's your fucking soul mate, and you've made her wait long enough. Take her."

I frowned, torn between anxiety and excitement. "What if she doesn't want me?"

He rolled his eyes. "Please. The woman's been practically panting over a single image of your eyes in her memory for a year, not including all the naughty little fantasies you two have been living together in your dreams. Don't pretend like you don't know about that, either. We're talking major fappage from the both of you. Aoife wants you; she feels that bond. You've got this if you'll just take it."

"And what, you're just going to walk away?"

He laughed. "Oh, honey. First of all, I'm the bestie, which means I'm not going anywhere. You and I will be getting to know each other real well. And second, you're more my type than she is...by far. I'm as queer as a three-dollar bill, and that little lady has known it since the day we met. Now, if you'll excuse me, beefcake, I'm going to head off with this lovely precog witch to work on seeing the upcoming battle. It's easier to strategize when you know what the opposition is going to do, and we've got about ten hours before the shit hits the fan."

He strode down the hall with Amber by his side, waggling his fingers at me before disappearing around the corner.

"Jackass," I yelled, which only made him laugh. As I turned

around, I caught the eye of Rex, who stood watching me with Bez, Sandman, and Lanie.

"What?" I barked.

Rex shrugged. "Nothing, man. Just thinking how I'd already be halfway to wherever my mate was if I'd gotten the green light like that."

I opened my mouth to speak, but the words never came. Fuck my pride...I needed to find my woman and make sure she knew she was exactly that. Mine.

I spun and jogged down the hall, following my mate's scent. On the hunt for a necromancer. On the hunt for *my* necromancer.

SIX

"HE WASN'T AFRAID OR in pain," I said, looking at the man named Rebel with as much honesty as I could. "He wasn't concerned about his own death at all; he was more worried about someone named Blaze."

Rebel didn't respond. He wasn't even looking at me, choosing instead to glare at the window on the far side of the room. Not that I blamed him. Death was never easy to deal with.

"That's the leader," Charlotte, a blond woman who clung to Rebel's side, whispered. She'd been at the campground and had crossed the river with a large, buff-colored wolf. I assumed that wolf was Rebel. "Blaze is President Blasius Zenne. He runs the North American Lycan Brotherhood from here. We're supposed to be celebrating his birthday this weekend."

I nodded. "Numbers must have truly respected him. It was clear in his words and the concern he showed for the man."

"Is he dead?" Rebel asked suddenly, still staring out the window. "Is the fucker who killed Numbers dead?"

Gates answered for me from where he stood against the wall. "Yes. I took care of it, boss."

"Good." Rebel looked away from the window, his pained, blue eyes meeting mine. I knew that look, had seen it a hundred times before. He felt helpless. Someone he cared about had been taken from him, and the retribution he needed to soothe the ache of his loss wasn't going to happen.

Seeing people wearing expressions like that were what I hated about speaking with the dead. Sometimes, I was able to truly help a person heal. To make sure one soul went on to the land of the dead while those left behind found peace and acceptance. But that was the good side. The bad side was looking at people like Rebel—people who needed closure and would never find it. Who were having trouble dealing with a sudden and often violent death of someone around them.

I wrung my hands in my lap and struggled to find the words that could ease his pain. Not that I'd ever found them before. I'd been dealing with living relatives and friends for years and still seemed to get this part wrong. But before I could say anything that would embarrass me or make Rebel mad, the doors to the study opened and a young man entered.

"Char?"

Charlotte turned and smiled. "Right here, Julian."

He walked in slowly, carefully, leading with a white and red cane. "I'm hungry. Want to grab a snack with me?"

"Why don't we all go?" She looked up at Rebel, rubbing his arm. He tried to smile, but it fell, making hers dim as well. "Come with us. I don't want to leave you alone."

Rebel paused, eyes locked on hers. So much anger and pain on his face, so much worry. And then he nodded. As the shifters and their significant others gathered in the center of the room, I stood and turned for the opposite set of doors. This was family time, time for them to mourn and begin the healing process. My job was done.

"I hope I was able to help," I said. The group turned as one to look at me, wolf and human alike. The hair on the back of my neck stood up as my instincts kicked in. I was in a room full of predators, and I was just weak enough to be prey. I needed to track down Jameson and get my bow back. "I'm going to go find my friend."

"Absolutely." Rebel stepped my way, reaching out to shake my hand. "Thank you for telling me about Numbers."

"Of course."

Charlotte smiled from Julian's side. "Are you sure you can't join us?"

"I'm sure, but thank you. Enjoy your snack." I hurried out of the room and into a long, opulent hallway, taking a deep breath. They seemed like nice people but, in a group, they made me nervous. Too many sharp teeth and animal mannerisms. I needed to escape for a few minutes.

Not far down the hall, I found a small alcove perfect for hiding. I scurried inside, my heart racing. Leaning my head against the wood wall in front of me, I took a few deep breaths and focused on calm. What a day. Men who shifted into wolves, witches, deaths, fires, walking under a cemetery, and meeting the man I'd been fantasizing about for a year. It felt as if I'd been awake for a week already, and it wasn't even dinnertime yet.

"You okay?"

I jumped and spun, my hand going to my chest.

"Fuck," I hissed. My stomach made a happy, jumpy sort of flip at seeing Jameson standing there. My God, up close he was even more stunning. His hair had dried, leaving it lighter with golden ends, making his eyes seem even bluer. And his smell. It was exactly as I imagined in my mind...imagined, or remembered. Having him this close, reliving all those sexy memories that technically never happened, made me crave contact. Fuck, I wanted him in the worst way. Wanted to relive all the wild and sweet moments in my mind. I just wanted.

But he didn't have the same recollections as I did. I'd spent the last year alone, refusing to let another man or woman touch me, only finding pleasure by my own hand to the thoughts of what he'd do to me if he were real. He hadn't.

The very real Jameson stared, his light eyes trapping mine.

I clenched my hands into fists, resisting the urge to touch. Fighting my own instincts.

"I wasn't expecting to see you," I said, my voice soft…too soft. "Is there something you need?"

The damned look he gave me… I'd kissed that wicked little smirk off his face a thousand times. Not doing so made me ache.

"I need a lot of things." He stepped closer, blocking my way out. "You seem a bit jumpy. You don't have to be afraid of us…or me."

I licked my bottom lip and pulled it between my teeth for a moment, wanting so badly to do the same to his. "No. Not afraid."

He nodded, eyes still on mine, inching into the alcove. "Wouldn't be wrong if you were. There're a lot of shifters running around."

"Shifters don't scare me," I whispered, the half-truth falling easily from my lips. Because while shifters scared me, he didn't. Not at all. No, he made me shake and shiver and whimper, but definitely not in fear.

"Good. That's good." He crept closer and lowered his voice. "My name's Jameson."

"I know. I'm Aoife."

"I know." Closer still, invading my space as he stared me down. Hunting me. "You're a necromancer."

"Yup. Born and bred that way. Me and the dead—" I held up my hand and crossed two of my fingers "—we're like this."

He nodded, fighting back a smile.

I grew serious and leaned back against the wall. Ready to put a few things out on the table. "You're a wolf shifter."

He smirked. "Yeah. Born and bred that way."

I gave him an irritated look, but his smile only grew. A cocky, arrogant smile that did strange things to my heart and other places in my body. I took a deep breath, pulling his scent inside of me, basking in it. I thought he'd move closer, maybe press himself against me—wished for it, really—but instead, his smile fell.

"I'm really sorry."

My brow tightened, furrowing. "For what?"

"For last year. For leaving you in that warehouse." He looked away, but not before I glimpsed that angry expression once more...that angry expression that suddenly looked more pained. "I thought you were dead."

I held my breath, ignoring the pain his words caused, the way my chest seized at the memory of it. But underneath that ache was something brighter, warmer. Something much like hope. He remembered me.

"I was in the land between, not dead." I stared up at him, open and ready to be truthful. "Sometimes, I thought you were a dream...but your eyes have haunted me ever since."

"Every day," he growled, moving closer, his warmth wrapping around me, leaving only millimeters between us. "You've been on my mind and in my dreams every fucking day. Torturing me."

Finally, he closed the space between us, his chest brushing mine. The touch of his body setting mine on fire. "It confused me. I've touched every inch of your body in my dreams, but I thought you were dead. I never would have left you if I'd known there was any way..."

And that was the moment when my heart nearly stopped. All those months, this past year, I'd been dreaming about a man who I thought hadn't wanted me. Believing he'd left me behind. Hell, not even believing he was real at times. But he *was*, real and here and talking to me. Seducing me with his closeness and his words. And I loved it.

"Thank God I was wrong." My whisper sounded breathy even to my own ears, not that he seemed to mind. Tired of waiting, I hooked a finger into the belt loop of his jeans, tugging lightly. Wanting to pull him closer. Needing to *feel* him. He leaned to brush his nose against mine. A simple touch, but one that made sparks shoot up my spine. Shaking inside. Craving more.

"Jameson?"

"Yeah?" His breath ghosted over my cheek, making me shiver.

"I'm glad you finally found me." I pulled, drawing him to me, surrendering to the want within.

He huffed a laugh, letting his body press against mine, a low growl sounding from his chest. "Pretty sure you found me, beautiful."

I leaned my head back as he nuzzled into my neck. Shivering, reaching to grab his arms. He placed a single, soft kiss to my collarbone then lifted his head, meeting my eyes again.

"What are you doing?" I asked, breathless.

"Manning up." He leaned closer, lips almost too close to mine, breathing my air.

"Did Percy tell you to do that?"

A pause, a growl, and then a sigh. "Yeah. He did."

I ran my hands up to his shoulders. "He is *such* a good friend."

Jameson chuckled, his hands skimming my hips, my waist, up my rib cage, only to turn around and retrace their path. "I'm beginning to think so as well."

I sighed, wanting more, needing him to touch me. Kiss me. Grab me. Something. Anything. But instead, he pulled back, staring down at me as he grew more serious. As his hands stilled.

"You're my mate," he whispered. So intense. As if afraid of the words.

"Okay." I nodded and took a deep breath to recenter myself, trying to stay focused. "What does that mean?"

Jesus, the look he gave me. So much warmth in it, so much need. He was pure, animalistic desire, and I was eating it up.

"It means you're meant for me, and I'm meant for you. It means, if you'll let me, I'll devote my life to you. I'll take care of you, protect you, do everything in my power to make you happy. It means fate put us together for a reason." Leaning to place a kiss to my jaw, he moaned and opened his mouth on my chin, biting down a little. Like a warning. Or a promise. His tongue soothed the teeth marks when he released me. "It means I want you."

"What about you?" I asked, digging my nails into his biceps. He grunted and pressed even closer, pinning me against the wall. Letting me feel every inch of his body along the length of mine. Teasing me with his heat and his strength.

"What *about* me?" he asked, growling low and steady.

"What about what you want?" I let my head fall back against the wall as he slowly licked and kissed up my neck. Things were going so fast, so blazingly quick, but they felt right. He felt right. And his body certainly felt right. "Do I get to take care of you, protect you, and make you happy?"

He jerked back, his growl deepening, eyes practically blue fire. I refused to look away, knowing what I wanted…what I needed. What I craved.

"What would make you happy right now, Jameson?"

He stared down at me, that fire inside him burning out of control as his hands slid to my hips and grabbed. Hard. "You. I've been dreaming of you for a year, Aoife. Every day, every night. You've been with me this whole time."

I died. Not literally, but the woman I'd been for the past year—the one who cried for something she'd lost, who convinced herself over and over again that this man couldn't be real, who locked herself off from just about everyone to hole up and live in a fantasy world—died. Jameson was here and real; I was not going to waste a single moment doubting myself when it came to him.

"You want me?" I asked, shifting my hip against his erection, teasing him, wanting to hear the words.

"Fuck, yes," he growled, rocking back into me, bringing his knee between my thighs to press against where I was already so wet and hot for him. Oh God, the growl. It vibrated through my body, teasing me, making me gasp as every part of me craved to feel that sound, as I pressed myself down on his thigh, not wanting to stop. Needing more. Wanting him to take. Knowing he needed a little push.

So I rose onto the balls of my feet, letting my lips barely brush his. And I whispered, "Prove it."

And, by God, the man proved it.

He pressed me against the wall, lips crashing into mine with a force just this side of painful, kissing me in a way that spoke of lust and desire, of possession and want. He kissed me like a man dying to be kissed, and I kissed him back just as hard. There was no softness in the act, no newness or tentative fumbling. Neither of us needed sweet and gentle. Our first kiss had been a year in the making, had been played out between us a thousand times already. Our first kiss was a taking, a desperate attempt to merge two souls into one with our mouths.

I clung to his shoulders, rising higher, desperate to be taller. He must have understood what I needed because he slid his hands under my ass and lifted me, pinning me to the wall by my hips. The position placed his very hard, very thick cock right in between my legs, exactly where I wanted him to be. Sans the layers of clothing between us, of course.

"Damn, I love when you do that," I gasped as he moved to my jaw. Biting. Licking. Sucking. Fuck, he was going to leave a mark, and I was going to love it. I'd show it off like a badge of honor.

"I remember," he grumbled, shifting his hips to press against mine as he sucked hard on my collarbone. Fuck me, this man didn't know the meaning of the word gentle, and I thanked whatever fate brought us together for that fact.

"That wasn't real then," I said, practically panting. "But it is now." I wrapped my legs around his hips and used my thighs to pull him in, squeezing his cock between us, pressing him where I was desperate to feel more. He hissed and pulled his mouth off my body, his head dropping as our hips quickly found a rhythm. Rocking against one another. Teasing.

"Fuck, Aoife. You're killing me. I was only coming to talk to you."

I giggled, which turned into a moan when he thrust his hips hard and fast. "Talking's overrated. And if you think this is killing you, wait until you get me naked."

He growled louder, pressing harder, kissing me soundly. I was ready to tell him to find us a room, to strip him down and do whatever we wanted to do, but a chill went down my spine right as a screech sounded through the air. I pulled away with a gasp, turning my head to look down the hall. The view shimmered, lights sparking along the edges of my vision.

"Damn it," I hissed, dropping my head to Jameson's shoulder. He growled and set me down, keeping his hands on me and his body in front of mine.

"What's wrong?"

"They're coming."

He growled louder, turning to look. "Who?"

"The dead…through the cemetery. The spirits are restless and trying to reach me."

"They can get to you this far away?"

"Only when they really want to." I met his concerned eyes. "They don't like the energy around the men outside. They're disturbed by it."

He brought his hand to my face, traced the line of my

cheek like he'd done in my fantasies a hundred times. My heart swooned at the memory, collecting pieces of the real and not real and fitting them together.

"What can I do?"

"We should probably go and join the rest of the group," I said, hating every word as it came out of my mouth. "More people around me will help stave them off."

"All right." He took a step back before closing his eyes and looking to the floor. "Just...give me a second."

I waited, breathing hard, until I couldn't wait any more. "Are you okay?"

"Yeah, just..." he sighed, shrugging. "You've been grinding on my dick for the past five minutes. I need a second to get the blood back in my brain."

I smiled, biting my lip to keep that from moving into grin territory. "Sorry, I guess."

"Don't apologize for that...ever." He opened those gorgeous blue eyes, meeting mine, trapping me in his gaze once more. "I'm actually sort of glad for the interruption, though."

"Why?" I asked as he grabbed my hand and pulled me with him down the hall.

"Why, what?"

"Why are you glad to be interrupted?"

He gave me a look, one filled with fire and intensity. One that made my toes curl. "Because in another few seconds, I'd have started stripping you right there in the hall."

I nodded, opening my eyes wide, slightly mocking. "God forbid we get naked."

"Hold up." He curled his arms around my waist in the middle of the hall and pulled me tight against him. "I really *was* coming only to talk to you. I've thought you were dead for the past year, and I don't want to wait a single second to claim you as mine. But I also understand how new this is and how little you actually know about this life and me. I don't want to push you."

"Push me how?"

His brows came down, making him look adorably confused. "I don't want to push you to move too fast. Pressure you into something you're not ready for. I've been living with you in my head as my lover and mate for a year, but I don't want to make assumptions about how you feel or what you want from me, if anything. If you're willing to get to know me, we can go at your pace."

I laughed, unable to stop myself. "Oh Jameson, you weren't pushing me at all. I only meant good on the interruption because I gladly would have let you strip me naked right there in the hall."

He stared at me, jaw hanging open. I smirked and sidled up to him, rising up to bite his lip before whispering against his mouth.

"I saw you in my head as well, Jameson. I've been tortured by your ghost fingers and mouth more times than I can count, woken up sweaty and tingling nearly every morning, gone through more batteries than any woman rightfully should in ten years let alone one." I scratched my hands down his chest, grabbed the waistband of his jeans, and pulled him to follow me as I backed down the hall. "You won't be pushing me because I've been fucking you in my mind every day for a year. I'd really like to try the reality, though. So next time, we should start in a room so we have a little privacy. No one needs to see what I plan on doing to you when I finally get you alone."

SEVEN

"SOMETHING WRONG, WORKER BEE?" Moira smiled wickedly, her eyes glinting with mischief as Aoife and I walked past her into the front parlor. I glowered at the woman, keeping it more sarcastic than harsh. The troublemaker.

We'd met outside this very room, not long after she'd come home with her new mates. I'd caught her hiding across the hall, too unsure of her place in Blaze's life to ask for what she needed. So I'd pushed her while refusing to tell her my name, calling myself a worker bee. Of course, she remembered that moment well and tended to throw my little sarcastic comment back at me every single time I saw her. Moira was a strong woman, a good mate for Blasius and Dante, but she had a wicked sense of humor. And I tended to be at the receiving end of that more often than not.

"Behave, Moira." I ignored her chuckle and directed Aoife toward the couch on the back wall, hoping for a few quiet moments before we dove into planning. But a shout from across the room changed those plans.

"Hey, Aoife. Come here for a second." Percy waved at my mate from where he stood with Amber, as if he was some kind of ground traffic controller directing a plane to land. Irritating little fucker.

Aoife inched closer, clinging to my hand as if she didn't want to let go. I clung right back, pressing my side into her back to let her know I was there. To keep from grabbing her and running to my room, to my den, to a place we could hide together. I knew we were needed, that there was a lot of planning to do for tonight, but that didn't mean I wanted to spend a second without her. And yet, I didn't want her anywhere near the potential battle shaping up.

Fuck, this newly mated thing was hard to balance.

Eventually, Aoife sighed and looked back at me with a sad sort of smile.

"I'm being summoned." She moved as if to walk away, making my wolf howl in my head. Obviously, I wasn't done with her yet.

I pulled her to me, wrapped my arms around her for what should have been a quick hug, but became one that lingered, stretched into too many seconds. One that morphed into a full-body cuddle with me almost bent in half around her body. I caught Percy's sourpuss expression and returned a wolfish grin. Fuck his plans. I had my mate in my arms, and she was holding on to me just as tightly as I was to her. Percy could wait.

Moira's giggle made my mate jump and pull herself out of my arms. The president's mate got a growl from me in return. Refusing to be rushed, I leaned down to kiss Aoife's pink lips softly before letting her go with a slap to her ass.

"Hurry back."

She gave my hand one final squeeze before heading toward her friend, hips swaying with every step. I watched her go, my heart tightening, my groin as well. Damn, my mate was beautiful. But as she moved farther away, out of my reach, worry niggled at me. The weight of it kept me from focusing completely on the other people in the room. Kept my eyes tracking her body, and not just because she had an ass I wanted to bite.

She was going to fight alongside us, and that made me crazed.

I knew she had skills, had seen how she shot that bow with my own eyes, but she was my mate. A mate I thought I'd lost once. Living without her when I'd never met her had been agony; living without her now that I'd touched her, held her, tasted her lips… I didn't think I could survive it.

"Something we should know about?" Moira asked as she sidled up.

"Why do you ask?" I kept my eyes on Aoife, or rather, Aoife's ass. I couldn't help myself.

"Because you look like a sad little puppy."

I growled and gave her a sideways glare. "I'll show you a puppy."

"Ah, the worker bee has a weak spot." She laughed, tilting her head as she looked to where my girl stood. "So shall I assume the young necromancer is your mate?"

The smile that spread across my face was automatic and impossible to stop. And my voice when I answered her was one filled with pride, with appreciation, with gratitude.

"Yes, Aoife is my mate." As if she heard my words, Aoife chose that moment to glance across the room, catching my smile. Her returning one was just as wide, her cheeks tingeing pink before she returned her attention to her conversation.

"She's lovely." Moira stepped in front of me, meeting my eyes for the first time in our conversation. "She's also very talented with that bow, from what I hear. A warrior of sorts. She's a good fit for you."

My stomach sank along with my smile at the mention of Aoife and her bow. "Yeah, she is."

Moira's eyes narrowed. "You seem unsure of something. What's the problem?"

I swallowed hard before whispering, "She wants to fight alongside us."

She paused, watching me, obviously confused. "And?"

"She's essentially human."

"Well, yes," she answered, drawing out the words. "But she's strong and deadly with that bow of hers. Add the little psychic who assists her into the mix and I'm pretty sure she can take care of herself."

"But it's my job to take care of her." I stared after Aoife again, wishing to be next to her, wishing she didn't have to be in the middle of this. "Fuck, this is why mated guys shouldn't ride or fight."

My head spun as Moira snarled, punctuating her anger with a slap to my chest.

"You listen here, Jameson. Your idea of taking care of your mate seems a bit antiquated, so let me give you an update. She's not some weak little damsel in distress, nor is she unable to care for herself. She's strong, independent, and perfectly willing to fight on her own behalf. She doesn't need you to coddle her."

I took a step back. "I wasn't going to—"

"Yes, you were." She followed me, forcing me to retreat further, her finger poking my chest. "You were going to say how the man has to be all strong and protective while the woman runs and hides. As if she's going to falter during the fight simply because she has a vagina."

"Moira, no—"

She waved her hand, fanning her face, raising her voice to some kind of overly feminine level. "Oh dear, those big, bad men over there scare me. I think I've gone and caught a case of the vapors."

"The what? No, I—"

She pushed forward, snarling loudly through her words. "Even though she can handle herself, you don't want her on that field. You don't want her to use her skills to fight. You don't want her anywhere near the battlefield. Admit it. If it were up to you, she'd probably be locked away in a safe room right now."

I growled, tired of feeling under attack for caring about my mate's safety. "If she fights, I'll be worried about her. My head won't be clear, and I won't be able to concentrate on what needs to get done."

Moira cocked her head and crossed her arms. "Seems like that's your issue, not hers."

I opened my mouth to answer, but nothing came out. How could I argue her words when they were true? Aoife could defend herself; she'd even protected me at the campground. And yet, I hated the thought of her outside in the fight. I wanted her safe, protected. Sheltered.

And...fuck.

Before I could say anything, Angelita, the young Omega Bez had rescued when he met his mate, padded into the room, making a beeline for us through the crowd. The little wolf nudged Moira's hand with her wet nose and whined. Meeting those dark, deep canine eyes, my stomach dropped almost to my knees. She was why we fought, why we raged, why we killed ourselves to find the rest of the Omegas in danger. She was why Aoife needed to be outside with us.

The little wolf stared, almost challenging, her eyes filled with what I swear was irritation. So now I'd pissed her off as well. Wonderful. The women seemed set on ganging up on me, even though I was ready to admit they were probably right.

Moira sighed, backing away. "Look, Jameson. I know being mated to someone is new to you, but let me give you a hint. No woman wants to be treated like glass. Yes, she's basically human and, therefore, a bit more fragile than a shifter, but she's not helpless. My mates are both man enough to allow me to make my decision, which is why I'll be inside the mansion during the fight doing what I can to protect those who can't protect themselves. I believe your mate would appreciate the same respect. Don't treat her as if her strength and skill has no value or you'll do nothing but push her away."

Angelita growled low, a sound I took as agreement with Moira. Piling on the guilt.

"Ready to go?" Moira asked the wolf, her voice softer than when she'd been scolding me. Angelita whined, to which Moira nodded. "Fine. If you'll excuse us, Jameson. I need to make sure Angelita has some time to run around before tonight. She's neither old enough nor experienced enough to fight, in my opinion. I suggest you remember your mate is both."

She and Angelita gave me strong, disapproving looks before walking away. I watched them leave, my thoughts in a spiral. My mate—who I'd thought was dead—was very much alive. She was also very much in a body that could be damaged easily. Yet Aoife was strong enough to kill shifters with nothing but her bow and arrows. A near impossible feat, really, considering we'd have to basically bleed out to stop our natural regeneration.

I hadn't thought much about it at the campground, too obsessed with her just being alive, but she'd shot wolves and killed them. One shot, one arrow, dead. A simple wound like that shouldn't have been able to knock us down for long. Those wolves should have gotten back up and healed within minutes. Yet they hadn't—they'd lay on the ground, bleeding into the grass. Giving up. Unwilling or unable to get back to their feet. Impossible.

"Something on your mind?"

I spun to find Aoife behind me, bathing me in her scent and calming my nerves. A little. Still, something wasn't fitting right about what I'd seen at the campground.

"Nothing beyond the normal stress of an upcoming battle." I grabbed her hand, unable to deny my urge to touch her. Overwhelmed by my desire to make her mine.

She stepped into my hungry arms, placing her head on my

chest with a quiet hum. "What's with the dog?"

"She's a wolf." I ran my hands up her back and curled my body over hers, resting my chin on her head.

"She's smaller than the rest of you...or at least the wolves I've seen."

"She's young still. Just turned sixteen." I breathed deep, inhaling her scent, wishing for a few moments of peace and privacy. "The men outside murdered her pack, her family, and kidnapped her."

Aoife lurched back, eyes wide. "Jesus."

"Yeah, it was one of the worst attacks on a pack we've ever seen. Angelita, the little wolf, was rescued by that guy over there" —I pointed at Bez— "and now lives with him and his mate."

"But she's stuck in her wolf form, unable to shift human." Aoife bit her lip, her eyes a little watery. "Forever?"

I pulled her close once more. "No. Just until she learns to control her wolf side. Teenage hormones and shifting are a volatile combination. Most of us Borzohns have gotten stuck a time or two."

Aoife ran a finger over my collarbone as she asked, "What's a Borzohn?"

"Born. Some of us are born with our wolf spirits inside; some of us are made or turned from human to shifter."

"Oh." Aoife kept staring at my neck, unfocused.

"Something on your mind?"

She smiled, a soft, sweet one that made my heart thump and my cock harden. "No, not really just..."

I waited for her to finish her statement, but instead she continued to stare, her attention completely absorbed by something else. "Aoife, what's up?"

She sighed. "Death follows the little wolf."

"What was that?" Bez's gruff voice made Aoife jump. I spun, facing the outraged shifter down as I moved Aoife slightly behind me.

"Bez," I growled.

He ignored me, glaring hard at Aoife. "What did you say about my ward?"

Aoife looked from me to Bez, clinging to my arm as she murmured, "Death follows her. He dances around her."

"Excuse me?" Bez stalked forward, ignoring my warning growl and focusing on my mate. "Did you say she's going to die?"

"No, no, that's not what I said. Not at all." Aoife glanced at me, eyes wide and skin flushed. Then she sighed. "She's seen too much, been too close to it. Death has gotten a taste of her soul, and he doesn't like to give up something as sweet as a young innocent." She raised her hand, making small tracing motions with her fingers. "But there's a field around her, sort of like a shield. Death can't go through that. He'll keep trying, but he won't succeed until it's her time. She is…oddly protected."

Bez stepped back, brows drawn down over his light eyes. "Oh."

"Yeah, oh." Aoife moved toward him, a soft, patient expression on her pretty face. "It's hard to explain or understand sometimes, the way Death works. But he's clear to me on this one—he wants her, and he can't get to her. Keep her out of trouble; keep her cognizant of the fragility of life. She won't be bulletproof forever, and there's no way to know when that shield will fall. But for today, she's safe."

Bez nodded once, still in protective mode. Still growling. "While I appreciate the words," he said, glaring hard at my mate, "I'd appreciate it more if you stayed the hell away from Angelita."

"Bez," I growled, warning.

He shook his head. "I'm happy for you, man; I really am. But there are questions around your little necromancer. I don't want her near Angelita."

Before I could even growl, Aoife nodded.

"Whatever you prefer. I'm not here to cause trouble."

"We'll see about that. Meeting with Blaze in two minutes in the library. I suggest you two not miss it." He glared down at Aoife before turning on his heel and striding away. I watched him leave, my mind spinning with all the questions. And yet, when Aoife sighed as if he'd hurt her feelings, nothing mattered but making her smile again. I pulled her into my arms and kissed her, a deep, soulful kiss I just couldn't resist.

"What was that for?" she asked when it was done, eyes bright as they met mine.

"Nothing, really," I lied, unable to put my feelings into words other than want, need, crave, and please. "Just needed a reminder of your taste."

"Hmmm." She rose up, kissing me back. "Maybe we could find a little time alone, before we have to get ready for the fight."

My cock ached for her, my body tight and ready. I growled, nuzzling her nose and pressing my hard cock into her hip so she could feel my desire. So she knew how much I wanted her.

"Let's get this meeting over with. I want time with my mate."

EIGHT

Aoife

AMBER APPROACHED ME IN the hall, pulling me away from Jameson. He didn't seem to like being separated from me, not that I did, but I smiled and shooed him into the room. The witch seemed to have something on her mind.

"I don't mean to be forward," she said, wringing her hands. "But I was curious about your power."

"Like, how it works?"

She shrugged. "More what you can do. Percy said you're a necromancer, but it sounds like you might be more. Are you a medium?"

"A medium speaks to the dead, or the dead speak through them. Depends on your definition. I, as a necromancer, see the dead, feel them, *and* hear them. I can also travel to the land between the living and the dead to help them find their way through when needed."

Her eyes went wide, slightly unfocused. "Huh, so more death speaker than medium."

"I don't know what a death speaker is."

"Never mind," she said, refocusing on me. Looking more energized than before. "It's a term we use as witches to categorize the level of access to the dead. Traversing realms and planes of existence puts you at the top level, the most powerful. Your gift is rare."

"So I've heard."

"I'm not helpful, am I?" She smiled, showcasing a dimple that made her appear younger somehow. "Go on, Aoife. I believe your red thread is waiting for you."

"Red thread?"

"Soul mate. Your one and only love." Her smile fell a little, seeming more forced than before. "Not everyone finds theirs, or they do and something gets in the way. But you and Jameson are going to have an amazing life together. I'm sure of it."

My neck and cheeks burned as I grinned, unable to hold back either reaction. "I hope so. We just have to make it out of here alive, right?"

Amber bit her lip and grabbed my hand, staring over my shoulder as her eyes went unfocused once more. "Deserts at sunrise are beautiful, especially from your soul mate's back porch. You have many more to see, death speaker."

With a wink, she released my hand and walked through the door to the library, leaving me a bit off-balance. Having dealt with Percy for most of my life, I was used to cryptic statements and promises of a future. But this was different...desert sunrises and back porches? What the hell had she seen?

As Blaze called the group to order, I slipped into the room and to Jameson's side. Needing to be close to him. Wanting to feel his touch. He obliged, wrapping an arm around my shoulders as Blaze talked about strategy and defensive lines. Things that pretty much went in one ear and out the other. I was too busy concentrating on the way Jameson's skin felt against mine.

"We have a solid plan in place," Blaze said loud enough for the entire room to hear and interrupting my fantasizing about Jameson and me doing dirty things back in that alcove. But how could anyone blame me? The man was delicious in every sense of the word.

Blaze shuffled his papers, collecting them into a pile before glancing to where Percy and Amber stood along the windows. "We also have a few hours before the fight begins, yes?"

Percy nodded. "Yeah, not until the moon is high. A little over nine hours, we believe."

"Then I suggest we use the time for preparation. I'll start with Bez and his team, then add in others as we work through strategy." Blaze glanced over the room, giving each man and woman an individual look, his eyes guarded when they met mine. "Stay reachable, don't go outside, and be prepared for anything. You're all dismissed."

Before the last word fully left his lips, Jameson grabbed my hand and dragged me out the door, rushing down the hall toward the basement steps.

"Where are we going?" I asked, laughing at his eagerness. Not that I cared. My entire body felt electrified, as if I'd been shocked from my fingertips to my toes. Energized and ready for some kind of release, one I knew only he could bring about. I would have followed him anywhere.

"Downstairs...my room." He growled, all beastly and strong. The things that sound did to me were ridiculous—his growl was straight-up foreplay.

"But shouldn't we stay around in case they need us?" I asked, not really caring too much about the preparations for tonight. I'd rather spend a few quiet moments alone with my dream man while I had him. Death roamed the halls, but he wasn't strong enough to overpower my need. Not this time. Though he did make me pause.

"We'll be available if needed." Jameson gave me a surprisingly soft look over his shoulder. "But right now, I want you alone."

"Jameson." I stopped, desperate to touch him but knowing the timing was bad. Fighting with myself to do what was right for the group and not just me. No matter how much I desired him, there was no way I should put my need for…something… above our safety. Even though I wanted to. Wanted whatever the *something* was. Badly.

Jameson watched me, solid and sure and still. I fidgeted, growing hotter under that look, the need to touch him intensifying, the uncomfortable tingle in my skin aching until I made a sound like a whimper. He yanked me into his arms, pulling my feet off the ground with the strength of his hug and wrapping his entire body around me. I clung to him, suddenly shaky, the feel of him against me like a balm to my anxiety.

We stood that way for minutes on end, holding one another right there in the middle of the hallway, not speaking. Jameson spent the time shushing me, calming me by running a hand down my hair, breathing with me. I tucked my head into his neck and surrendered to his touch. The craving, the desperation within me for this man, was out of control. I'd never felt anything like it, and I didn't know how to explain it except for one word. Need. I needed to feel him. I needed to be with him. I needed skin on skin.

"Listen, beautiful," Jameson whispered, his warm breath making me shiver. "Do you hear them?"

I strained my ears, trying to hear what he did. Trying to hear anything but my own heartbeat. At first there was nothing, but then—

Thumping. Grunting. Moaning.

"Oh my God." I pulled back, my wide eyes meeting his calm ones. "Someone's having sex!"

Jameson growled deep, the sound vibrating against my chest. "Yeah, they are."

"But we have a war to fight."

"All the more reason. Who knows if we'll all survive? Sex is the physical display of their emotions. Whoever that is, they're expressing their care and concern for their partner with their bodies." He leaned down and kissed me, soft but deep, the way I loved to be kissed, leaving me breathless when he finally released my lips. "I want to show you how much you mean to me, how beautiful and sexy I think you are. How a shifter treasures his mate. I want to actually live the memories we have between us. Will you let me do that?"

"Jameson," I sighed as he nibbled my earlobe.

"Aoife." His hands slid down to my ass, pulling, squeezing in the manliest sort of way. A sort of claiming, of saying, "I own this" with just his hands. And he did. I'd known it for a year, felt it between us in every dream. He owned a piece of me, and I gave that up willingly because I owned a piece of him as well.

"Not here," I whispered when he pressed his hard cock against my stomach and flexed his hips. Jesus. I shimmied out of his arms, ignoring his growl of protest until I had my feet firmly on the floor, though his hand was still planted squarely on my ass. "I want to be alone with you."

"Good." He grabbed my hand again and led me to the basement, though this time there was no dragging. I followed willingly, excited and anxious in a good way for what was about to happen. I needed him, wanted him, and I'd never been one to deny myself something I craved. I was ready to give myself to him, to feel him on top of me, inside of me, as I had in my dreams for the past year. Ready to live out my fantasies.

When we reached what I had to assume was his room, he yanked me inside before slamming the door behind us.

"Fuck, I'm so crazed right now." He pushed up my shirt, not wasting even a moment to question what was about to happen. Thank God.

"Why?" I unsnapped his jeans and pushed them down his hips, clumsy and rough.

"I'm worried about you. I don't want you in the fight, but I want you beside me. I want to protect you, and I want you to go out there and kick ass because I know you can."

I grabbed his hips and pulled him close. "When anyone dies near me, I feel it. I know the moment their soul leaves their earthen body. I'd rather stand beside you and fight than cower in a corner while every death slaps me across the face. I don't want to worry that each one could be you."

"Fuck, Aoife." His groan turned to a growl as I bit his chest through his T-shirt. "I'm on fucking edge here. I don't think I can be gentle."

"Who said I needed gentle? Less talking, more—"

He didn't let me finish my sentence. His lips attacked mine in a kiss that set my soul on fire. They owned me, sucking, sliding, and moving in time with my own. I fumbled with his clothes, pushing his pants off his legs with my feet, yanking his shirt over his head. He stripped me just as roughly, tugging and pulling, literally tearing my panties from my hips. I stumbled backward out of his hold, pushing him away, trying to get a look at him, but he refused to release me. Growling, grabbing wherever he could, yanking me back into his hold. The moment was fierce, filled with desire bright enough to burn away any pain from such rough handling.

It was perfect.

I squealed when he lifted me, his thick fingers digging into the underside of my thighs. With a few quick steps, he placed me on the edge of the chest of drawers, forcing my upper body to recline as he loomed over me.

"I need to taste you." His breaths came fast, his words clipped and urgent. I nodded, leaning back, watching him as he stared. I rested on one elbow, drawing my legs up to place my heels on the edge of the dresser. With little more than a smile, I let my knees fall open. Inviting him.

"Go ahead."

A predatory leer spread across his face, a gleaming promise of what was about to happen.

"You sure about that?" His fingers traced my inner thigh,

up and down, making me shiver. Making me sigh. "I don't want to push you too far."

I linked our fingers together, dragging our joined hands toward where I was wet for him. "If you're not up for it, I can take care of myself."

Nearly moaning at the intensity in his eyes as they watched me, I slid our fingers down my stomach, over my hipbone. Farther, between my legs, pausing, making him wait for it. When he growled, I kept going, zeroing in on my clit. Rubbing over it, circling. Once, twice, then pulling him along as I slid two fingers inside. His deepening growl made me moan, made my hips buck and my head fall back. Made me plunge our fingers inside harder and faster.

"Fuck… Mine." He ripped my hand away from my flesh and dropped to his knees. Face hard, eyes burning, he attacked, licking me. Greedy and sloppy and perfect all at once.

"Oh, God." I rocked forward as he ran his tongue over my opening and back up to my clit. As he wrapped his lips around me and suckled. Toes curling, heart flying, I grabbed his hair and pulled. Hard. He growled against me, adding a vibration and making my orgasm come on faster and stronger than ever before. Sitting on the edge of the cliff, hanging on to that precipice between pleasure and pain, between more and stop. Waiting to fall. Holding my breath. Until, with his fingers inside of me and his lips firmly surrounding my clit, he growled again. Long and loud and so damn sexy, I crashed. Blissfully let go, let my body take over. I shivered all over, hissing curses, pulling his head against me. Riding it out on his tongue.

Jameson didn't stop. He kept licking and sucking me, teasing, leading me through every second until I finally had to push him away. Had to bring my knees together enough to block his access to the most sensitive parts of me. Instead of pulling back, though, he transferred his attention to my legs. Hands on my knees, he spread me once more, ignoring my whine, refusing to let me hide from his attention. But he didn't go too far, didn't attack my overstimulated clit. Instead, he worshiped my thighs. Kissing and licking his way up them. Biting his way back down from my knee. Squeezing my ample flesh, kneading it.

A nip, hard enough to make me jump, had him chuckling. "Do you know anything about shifter mating, Aoife?"

I answered breathlessly, still feeling slightly rubbery. "No. I didn't know about shifters until today. We'd never run into any before."

He hummed, snapping at my knee. Teeth meeting flesh for one hard, hot second. Fuck, who knew biting could be such a turn on?

"When a shifter finds their mate, their inner wolf demands to claim them."

I glanced down, nearly whimpering at the sight of him. His messy sex hair, his wet chin, his swollen lips. All from me.

"Claim them how?"

His teeth came down on my fleshy inner thigh as his hand held my hips still. Pushing me down. Demanding I stay in place.

"With a bite."

Well, that cleared my head a bit. "You want…to bite me?"

"I want us to bite each other." He left soothing kisses, small and soft, on my hipbones. "When you're ready."

I probably should have said no, brought up how little we knew about each other and how we just met and how much biting seemed like an odd choice to seal a commitment with. But my mind wasn't focused enough to block what my heart truly wanted. And what my heart wanted, what it had been consumed with for the past year, was him.

"Do it."

He pulled back, blue eyes questioning as they met mine. "Aoife?"

"Do it." I sat up, yanking him to me, kissing him, tasting myself on his lips. "Bite me, Jameson. Claim me."

He stared, growling low, looking so unbelievably torn. "It's permanent. There's no going back from a claiming bite. I'll be able to feel you, to track where you are. And you'll be able to feel me if you bite me back."

"I already feel you," I whispered, running my fingers down his chest and over the tip of his cock. Impatient. "I tracked you from Phoenix to Chicago. I felt drawn here, somehow knew you'd be here. That part's already in place. My soul is attached to yours, my heart owned. Take the rest. Take me."

His pause was miniscule, barely noticeable. But he made up for it. Grabbing me, wrapping my legs around his hips and picking me up, he carried me across the room. With great care, he placed me on the floor as he came back to my mouth. Kisses, harsh whispers, and hissed curses. All signs of his lust, of his urgency. Of how much he needed me.

He trailed his hand between us—down, down, down—until he could grab, hold himself ready. Eyes on his, I gave him a nod. No words needed. No more waiting. He slid into me with a single thrust, taking what he wanted. Giving me exactly what I needed. And I loved it. Loved having his weight on me, loved feeling the just-shy-of-painful slide of him inside. Loved his teeth against my collarbone as he thrust in and out. Loved the memory of him fucking me the same way he had been for the past year in my dreams.

"Jameson," I moaned, feet planted on the floor, lifting my hips to meet his thrusts. "Please."

His whining growl was the only warning I had before he clamped down on my neck. The bite was quick and hard, making me gasp, stinging for a single moment before a burn spread into my bones. And then my body seized, pleasure unlike any I'd ever known pulsing through me. Riding a wave so deep and wide, I couldn't see the end of it. Even my toes felt the ripple of the orgasm his claiming bite brought on. And then I was his. Completely, totally his. But I felt his emotions, knew that he needed more, that he needed me. Needed to become mine.

As my shaking calmed, I pushed on his shoulder, disconnecting us. He started to grab at me, to growl, but I shook my head and kept pushing. Forcing him to turn. Once I flipped him over, I crawled on top and slid him inside me once more. He groaned, head back, fingers gripping my hips in a way that made me hiss. Still, I dropped down, an inch or so at a time. Refusing to let him rush me. I lifted almost all the way off him, then dropped again. Lifted. Dropped. Going deeper with every pass. Relishing in his moans and growls, the way his eyes stayed locked on mine and his tongue came out to wet his lips.

Gorgeous.

"My turn." I rocked over him, hands on his chest, keeping him seated deep.

"Take what you want." He thrust up, lifting me. Making me gasp. So deep. I clawed at his chest, searching for purchase, trying to hang on as my legs quivered.

"A little more," I gasped, closing my eyes when he lifted me again. Damn, so good. I tilted my hips, leaning back, my hands on his thighs. Rode his thrusts as I rocked and squeezed. Let him lead even though I was on top. He was so deep like this, filling me so much, his strength making every second even better. I groaned, finger finding my clit, chasing a third high. Thrusting faster, gripping my hips, he jerked and stared at my hand as I rocked against it.

"Damn, Aoife."

I smiled, bringing my hand to his mouth, knowing exactly what he wanted. He sucked my fingers in all the way, growling around them, tasting me. Devouring me. Hair mussed from my fingers, face flushed, eyes wide and bright, he was so fucking handsome, so ready to come. Ready to be mine. And I was ready to take him.

"Does it matter where?" I shifted forward, circling my hips before lifting again, ready to take him over the edge. Ready to fall with him.

"I'm yours." His hands squeezed my thighs, holding me down for a second as he groaned. "Do what you want."

I nodded, restricting my motion even though he pouted. I lifted my hips, thighs shaking with the effort, forcing him to slow down, go at my pace. When he stopped pushing, went still as he watched me, I dropped down, taking him all the way back in. I leaned forward, kissing over his heart. Licking him. Whispering words of hope and promise into his skin as he gripped my legs, his hands clamped down in an iron-like vise. And finally, I bit him at the base of his neck.

His snarl was vicious, dropping low, shaking the ground. Head back, body stiff and hard, he screamed his pleasure to the world. To me. And then he grabbed my hips, pushing me off him. Flipping us, sliding back on top, thrusting hard into me, forcing me across the rug. My back burned and my hips hurt, but I liked it. Liked that level of pain. Liked seeing him completely lose himself to his orgasm. To the pleasure I gave him.

Shaking, moaning, huffing, he finally began to slow. Began to whimper and curse again. Holding himself deep inside, cuddling me closer, offering the warmth of his body. Snuggling us into a pile of exhausted, sweaty limbs. My heart slowed as we lay there, still connected, enjoying the peace with one another. The temporary peace.

"I'm so glad you found me," he whispered as he kissed my neck, tickling me.

I giggled, laughing harder when he grunted and finally pulled out of me. "I did find you, didn't I?"

"Totally." He pulled me closer, biting along my jaw. "In a hundred years when you're old and tired of me, I'm going to remind you that this is all on you."

"A hundred years?" I snorted. "You have high expectations."

He huffed, dropping his forehead against mine. "It's a mate thing, beautiful. You'll live longer because of me. We have lots and lots of time to get to know each other. Centuries even."

"Good." A kiss, a small one, even as my mind spun with this new knowledge. I was going to outlive my friends, the people around me, but I was going to be able to do it with Jameson by my side. Something I'd been desperate for since that day in the warehouse.

I sighed, cuddled closer, and brushed my lips against his cheek. "I feel like I've known you all this time. Like we've been together every day for this past year."

"I know this probably seems so fast to you, but we bonded that day. I felt the mating pull; I knew who you were to me. Every day since has been spent with you on my mind." He wrapped me tighter, whispering into my hair. "I couldn't stop thinking about you."

I hummed, loving the feel of him against me. Truly, really against me. No more dream man. This was Jameson, my mate and lover, in the flesh.

Reality was so much better than my dreams.

"This isn't fast," I whispered. "We've been together for a year—we just didn't know it."

NINE

Jameson

"FOOD."

Aoife's eyebrows rose. Not that I could blame her. I had my head resting on her hip while she laid hers on my thigh. Naked and alone for over four hours, we'd been having sex in one way or another almost the entire time. There were a year's worth of memories between us to recreate, and I'd done my best to cram in as many as possible in the short time we had. But that had backfired a little, leaving me starving.

"You want food, or you want to nickname *me* food?"

I ran my fingers up her inner thigh, teasing her, rubbing my thumb over her clit where my mouth had been only minutes before. "Well, I mean—"

"If you make a sexual eating joke right now, I'll kick you."

I chuckled and rolled on top of her, pinning her legs to the mattress, my chin in the perfect spot to tease her a little more. Something I couldn't resist. So I pressed down, rubbing in circles, my hands gripping her thighs.

She grabbed my hair, pulling, not really trying to make me stop but not egging me on, either.

"Jameson."

Fuck. I shivered, loving the way she said my name all breathy and sweet. Like she simply had to get the word out. Like she needed me to hear it.

Keeping her pinned, I moved down the mattress and ran my fingers up each side of her, pulling her open for me. She tried to close her legs, probably sore from how much time I'd already spent with my face buried in her sweet pussy, but I wouldn't let go. I licked her from bottom to top, giving that little clit a sweet kiss before I rested my head on her hipbone again. My thumbs still teased her, though. Unable to stop.

"Jameson," she groaned, almost whining, even as her legs shook.

"Yes, Aoife?"

She chuckled, which made me grin. "You said something about food."

My stomach growled, ready to eat itself. It'd been hours since my last meal, and I'd been burning through calories with Aoife. In a good way, but still—I needed to replenish. She probably did as well.

"I'm starving." I inched up her body, kissing over her flesh, my thumbs still sliding along each side of her pussy. "Let me make you dinner."

Her head jerked up so she could see me better. "You cook?"

"I'm over a hundred years old. Of course I cook."

Lying back, she watched me, her brow furrowed. "How much older?"

I sucked on the soft skin of her stomach, leaving a mark, loving the way she trembled beneath me as I did. "Hmmm?"

Sighing, bringing her hand to my face and holding me still, she replied, "How much older than one hundred are you?"

"Thirty-six years." I pushed down her body, staying out of her grasp as I licked across her hip to the seam of her leg. "I turned a hundred and thirty-six in June."

She lay gasping and moaning my name as I teased her,

kissed her, tasted her some more. I hadn't gotten my fill yet, and there were many more inches I had yet to love with my tongue.

But then she sighed a quiet, "Fuck."

"Okay." I crawled up her body again, biting her nipple as I brought my hips to meet hers.

"Not that, Jameson."

I pouted against her skin and looked up at her, meeting her smiling dark eyes. "What then?"

"Food."

My stomach growled again, louder this time. Aoife giggled, watching me, her hair all over the place and her face flushed. Beautiful.

"Right, food." I hopped up, kneeling on the bed, and holding out a hand for my mate. "I'm starving. Let me feed you."

IT TOOK US ANOTHER twenty minutes to leave my room. Aoife wanted to shower, and I wanted to fuck her against the shower walls when I saw her naked and wet. So I did. Still, once we made it to the cavernous kitchen I tended to prefer— the mansion had multiple options—my hunger for food took over. I picked the biggest, best-looking steaks from the walk-in refrigerator, grabbed some eggs, and carried all the ingredients I needed to make herb butter into the kitchen. Then I set to work. My mate needed to be taken care of, and I was definitely the man to do that.

As the broiler heated up, I chopped herbs at the island. Aoife sat on the opposite side. Watching me with a smile on my face. One that made my wolf and me proud because we'd put it there.

"What are you making?"

I shrugged. "Steak and eggs. A little herb butter to dress it up a bit. Simple, but protein packed to get us through the night."

She leaned forward, watching as I danced the knife through a pile of green. "What kind of herbs?"

I grabbed the softened butter and added it to a bowl, throwing the herbs in next, mixing as we talked. "Chives, thyme, and marjoram. I'm not picky about it usually, so I grab whatever's fresh and looks good."

"Huh." She sat back, her brow pulled down.

"What's up? You don't like something?"

"Oh no, I'm sure I will. I just...I don't cook like that."

I stopped mixing. "Like what?"

"Fancy." Her skin turned a bit pink, though I had no idea why she'd be embarrassed.

"Herbs are fancy?"

Her eyes met mine, dark and fiery, a pride there that said much more than words could. "When you're stocking up on ten-cent ramen noodles because all you need is water to make them, yeah. Herbs are fancy."

"Oh." I set the bowl down and frowned. "I didn't re—"

"Don't," she spat, harsh and final, leaving me off-balance and unsure. For as long as I'd known her in my mind, I knew nothing about her or her life. Apparently, there was plenty to learn...like the fact she struggled to make ends meet, or that she had a pride about her that wouldn't allow charity.

"Don't what?" I asked quietly, not wanting to upset her further.

"Don't apologize for my shitty life. Percy and me, we've made the best of it. It's hard because we both have so much trouble holding down a job, but we've always managed."

I tossed a towel over my shoulder and turned to put the steaks in the broiler, cursing myself again for walking out of that fucking warehouse last year. I could have been helping her, taking care of her. My wolf snarled *at me*, agreeing. We should have done so many things differently.

"I can't live on ramen, so when all this is done and we figure out what's next, expect steak in the freezer," I replied, knowing there'd be more than steak. Whatever she wanted, whatever she craved. My mate would have what her heart desired.

I didn't realize how quiet she'd become until I'd closed the oven door, grabbed the small frying pan, and been ready to crack an egg. When I turned her way, wondering what was up, she wasn't looking at me. In fact, she was staring at the island top, her body stiff.

"What's wrong?"

"I don't need to rely on you." Her voice was so soft, almost broken. And suddenly, I understood. I knew Aoife was strong enough to take care of herself, but what I hadn't thought about was how much independence came with that strength. I didn't want to take any of that away or overpower her. I simply wanted to help take care of her and let her take care of me. I wanted an equal…a partnership. Apparently, I needed to make sure she understood that.

"Hey." I leaned over the counter when she looked up, keeping my eyes on hers. "I never said you had to rely on me. I can't live on ramen because I'd burn through it too fast. Shifters eat a lot. I need protein. We also have voracious appetites for our mates. Even being this far away from you is torture. I want to drown in you, Aoife, but I can't do that if either of us is burning through our fuel source in a matter of minutes." I leaned a little farther, pressing my lips against hers before pulling back. "We get to take care of each other, remember? I'll buy us steak and cook it if you don't want to do it. You can clean up my mess."

She glanced at the counter, frowning. "But you didn't make a mess."

"I will if I know I don't have to clean it up." I winked at her. She rolled her eyes but grinned, something I was thankful to see again.

"Jackass," she said, running her fingertips over my hand.

"Your jackass."

"Totally."

I gave her one last kiss before spinning to check on dinner. Being here with her made me wish we were back in the desert at my place. Just the two of us. We could learn about one another, love one another, and be together without interruption there. I wanted to know everything about her, and I would. Once we finished this fight and could get away. Once I officially left the Feral Breed.

As soon as I cracked the eggs in the pan, I moved to the oven to check on the meat. The steak sizzled, fat melting as it cooked. Browning nicely.

"Almost done."

"I can't believe you're cooking for me."

I grinned and flipped her steak before moving back to the frying pan and the eggs. "We need to keep up our strength. I've got plans for you later."

Aoife laughed behind me, a sound I wanted to hear every day of my life, but I didn't turn around. My smile had fallen, worry taking over once more. I'd only just found her, just completed the mating bond with her. Fuck, we'd been naked together less than thirty minutes ago, and we would be fighting to keep our leader alive in the next few hours. Fighting to keep ourselves alive. Later might not come.

Without warning, her arms slid around my waist as she pressed herself against me. The effect of being wrapped in her was soothing, so I grabbed her hand and held her to me. Refusing to let go.

"You know," she said, her breath hot against my back even through the T-shirt I'd thrown on. "This whole mating bite thing is sort of freaky."

Turning her eggs, I frowned. "Freaky how?"

"Well, for instance, I know you're worried because I *feel* your worry. That makes me worry."

I pulled her hand to my mouth, kissing her palm, staring at the stovetop. "I don't want you to worry."

"I don't want you to worry either."

Moving the eggs onto a plate, I spun and grabbed her, pulling her off her feet and into my arms.

"I don't want you on the field," I growled, feeling my wolf close to the surface.

She frowned. "What?"

I bit back another growl, fighting internally to hold it together. "I want you to stay in the safe room with the other humans."

"No." Serious, final, no room for misjudging her words.

"No?"

"No. I'm able to fight, so I will."

"Aoife—"

"If I told you to hide, would you?"

"It's not hiding, it's staying safe." I cocked my head, eyeing her hard, giving up when she refused to budge. "Fine. No, I wouldn't. But I'm a shifter. There's not a lot that can kill me."

"Except other shifters, right? Exactly what we're going up against," she asked, her voice low, controlled. Warning.

I nodded, unable to find words to argue, still wanting to keep her safe but also understanding her point. I couldn't lock her away when I was in danger as well. I mean, I could, but she'd be pissed as hell at me, possibly for a long time. Maybe forever.

Aoife sighed. "Look, I get it. I'm just as scared of you being out on that field. But at least together, we have each other's back. I saved you at the campground; I can help you here as well. Stop doubting me."

She wiggled out of my hold so she could stand on her own again, making her point clear. "Don't burn the steaks, Jameson."

I huffed, giving up for the moment. "Right. Dinner."

"Yes, food." She didn't back down, didn't flinch, just stared with her head high. Waiting me out.

"I'm sorry," I said, shrugging. "I want you safe. I want you alive at the end of this. I want *you*. Forever."

Her face softened, her eyes going slightly watery. "I want you safe, too. But I'm not going to hide from a fight when I know I can help. Don't try to make me."

I nodded, understanding, leaning down for one final kiss. "I hear you, beautiful. And I'll do my best to listen."

"Thank you." She kissed me good and long, grabbing my ass to pull me against her. I dove into that kiss, moving with her, wanting to own some piece of her.

But too soon for my liking, she broke it and took a step back. "I wasn't kidding about the steaks."

"Tease," I growled, hungry for more than just food.

She left me alone with my thoughts—and an erection that practically wept for her attention—so I went back to cooking. And worrying. My opinion hadn't changed—I still wanted her locked away during the fight—but I didn't know if I could make that happen without seriously pissing her off. Or if I'd be able to make her understand why I did what I did once all was said and done.

Once I plated both our meals, we sat side by side at the island. Like any other couple enjoying a meal together. A moment of normal amidst all the crazy.

That first bite of steak, all hot and drizzled with the herb butter, made me groan. So good, so perfect after the day I'd had. Aoife ate with a passion that matched mine, humming and moaning with every bite. Distracting me from my food, a feat not many could accomplish. But her sounds were making me hard again, and I couldn't look away from her lips as she slid each bite between them.

"This is so good," she said, bringing another bite to her mouth.

I shifted on my stool, trying to find a more comfortable

position, my cock constrained in the jeans I'd thrown on. "Thanks, beautiful."

Another bite, a sigh this time, a look on her face that caused me to whimper. "You can really cook."

"Did you doubt me?" I asked, my voice low, my growl barely discernible but there.

She held up her fingers to pinch them together, scrunching her face in the most adorable way, making me want to kiss her pouty lips. "Maybe just a little bit."

Another bite of steak, another moan I could feel in my cock. I shifted again and dropped my hand to the fly of my jeans, pressing down, trying to relieve the pain.

"Fuck, Aoife. You have to stop that."

She peered at me, eyebrows raised, honestly having no idea the effect she had on me. "Stop what?"

"Stop moaning."

As my arm moved, she glanced down to where my hand rested in my lap. I ran the heel of my palm up the length of my cock, making it hurt, making it feel good at the same time. Showing her what she did to me.

"And if I don't?" she asked. Using her soft and breathy voice again. My kryptonite.

I growled hard, ready to take her. Wanting her more than my steak. "I'll make damned good use of this counter."

"Perhaps you could hold off on that, Jameson."

I whipped around as Blaze walked into the kitchen with Gates and Bez right behind him. Fuck me, talk about bad timing.

"Good evening, sir." I nodded their way.

He gave me a grim smile before focusing on my mate. "Miss Aoife. I don't believe we've officially met yet. I'm Blasius Zenne, president of the NALB."

Aoife looked from one man to another, her smile gone. Anxiety and nervousness shot through our bond, but she didn't show those emotions. Not to the men examining her.

"Hi. It's nice to finally meet you," she said, sounding confident and casual.

"Congratulations on your mating." Blaze glanced in my direction. "Jameson here is one of the best enforcers we have. I'll be sad to see him go."

Aoife frowned. "Go where?"

"He means when I leave the Feral Breed," I whispered, glaring. "Mated wolves don't ride."

"Keep telling yourself that," Gates said.

"Now, Gatekeeper. Just because it works for you and your den doesn't mean it works for everyone. The point is to have the choice whether to stay or go. Not to demand. Jameson has made his opinion on this matter known for many years, not just with the recent developments among Breed members." Blaze smiled, though it didn't reach his eyes. My wolf didn't like the energy coming from him either, or the way Gates stared at my mate.

"What's going on, guys?" I asked, inching back to keep my body between Aoife and Gates, ignoring his raised eyebrow when he noticed the move.

"We have a few plans to make," Blaze said, pulling a stool to the edge of the counter and sitting down. "But we've run into a slight problem that your Aoife might be able to help us with."

"What kind of problem?" I asked, aware of Aoife's hand on my back. Not sure which of us needed the contact more.

Bez approached the table, coming a bit too close to Aoife for my liking. "The kind of problem where wolves fall over and die with a single arrow shot from her bow."

He stepped as if to sneak past me, perhaps move to the other side of Aoife, but my low growl stopped him in his tracks.

"Where're you going, Bez?"

"Gentlemen," Blaze interjected from his seat at the end of

the counter. A spot that left plenty of room between himself and my mate. "This isn't an inquisition and we're not saying Aoife did anything wrong. The fact remains that she seems capable of putting wolves down who should be able to get back up, but they don't. I'd like to know how she does it."

I glanced at Aoife, ready to defend her, but she shook her head.

"My backpack has a cloth in the bottom that's been soaked in something called The Draught, as has the whole backpack, though not intentionally. That stuff transfers to my arrows whenever I store them in there."

Blaze's face went slack. "Excuse me?"

She glanced at me, reaching to hold my hand. Her anxiety skyrocketing to straight-up fear. "That day at the warehouse, the day you first saw me?"

I nodded, struggling to keep from grabbing her and running. Hating the fear she was throwing in my direction.

"I wasn't there by chance." She glanced at Gates out of the corner of her eye and squeezed my fingers. "I was working… for the Bastard Eights."

I snarled in surprise. The Bastard Eights was a human motorcycle club in the Flagstaff area, not quite one of the one-percent or criminal sort but close enough. Drugs and prostitution were their crimes of choice from what I'd gathered while investigating them. I'd been at the warehouse working as well, though for an entirely different reason.

"The guys who broke in to our denhouse?" I asked.

"Yeah," she said with a nod, her eyes going wide. "Though I didn't have anything to do with that. That was all some guy named Harkens."

Bez's head snapped back. "Harkens?"

"Yeah. Harkens Thearouguard. He came to the Eights with a deal. They would help him break in to a club in Flagstaff to snag the drug stuff so he could figure out how to make it, and he'd share it with them. He brought a sample of the drug to the warehouse the first time he came. The guys who took The Draught said they'd make a fortune selling it because it was a nice, smooth high. No letdown or panic."

"He gave The Draught to humans?" Blaze asked, a wicked fire in his eyes.

"Yeah. He had to prove the stuff wasn't just cranked-up aspirin or something." Aoife shrugged, casual, as if talking about drugs was a normal part of her day. My gut dropped when I realized it very well might be.

"How did you get involved?" I asked, gripping her hand, terrified to learn the rest.

She wove her fingers between mine. Hanging on. "Masterson."

"Masterson?" I asked, the name sounding familiar.

"Yeah, the leader of the vampires out there?" She swallowed hard as my eyes got bigger, my fear and fury ramping up. "Uh, well…vamps are essentially dead, so—"

"They're attracted to necromancers," Gates filled in for her. I growled, more at the thought of a vamp anywhere near my mate than at Gates.

"Exactly," Aoife said, rubbing her thumb over the back of my hand. Trying to calm me. "And old Masterson had a total obsession for a while there, no matter how many times I said it wasn't happening. I went to the Eights to see if they'd help get him off my back." She glanced at Gates, looking nervous. "I'd…done a few favors for them in the past. Not dealing or anything, just running product from one place to the other."

Gates stared at her, face stoic. "You worked as a drug mule."

She frowned. "Only when the ramen wasn't on sale or the electricity was about to get shut off. Percy and I, we try, but sometimes the money doesn't stretch as far as we need it to. It's hard to find work when a psychic gift you can't tell anyone about flares up in the middle of a shift and you have to leave to help someone, or a dead guy barrages you for days, making it so you can't hear anything else. When things got tight, I went to the Eights even though Percy hated it and refused to go with me. One of the guys was in foster care with us. I trusted him."

"A little boost to help you break free of a bad situation." Gates sounded softer than before, almost apologetic, which confused me. But Aoife seemed relieved.

"Exactly," she said, smiling at the shifter. "I didn't want to hurt anybody, but we had to keep a roof over our heads."

"Understandable." Gates nodded once, then frowned. "So Masterson was trying to…"

"Uh…" Aoife glanced my way, her cheeks darkening. "Let's say…date me?"

I snarled.

"Look, it's just the attraction between the dead in him and the necro in me," she said, rushing to get the words out. "Ghosts hit on me all the time."

"Not helping," I growled, gripping her hand tightly.

"So you asked your friend in the Bastard Eights for help," Blaze interjected. "But something went wrong."

Aoife nodded. "Masterson and his crew went wrong, yeah."

"They attacked?" Blaze leaned forward, his eyes bright, the intensity of his curiosity almost a living being around him.

"Not at first. Masterson and his two buddies came looking for me while I was at the warehouse. The Eights were trying to protect me, but things got physical."

"Physical…between humans and vampires," Bez said, his words slow and his voice overly calm. Vamps were as strong as shifters if not more so…there'd be no *getting physical*. There'd be a slaughter, which my gut told me was what had happened. And the aftermath was what I'd walked in on.

"Yeah. It wasn't much of a fight, really," Aoife said, frowning, confirming my thoughts. "One of the guys tipped over the brewing table during it, though, and a batch of The Draught went all over the floor."

"And your backpack," I added, assuming.

"Exactly. It coated the arrows inside. No matter how many times I wash the backpack, the residue lingers. Though it's a good thing."

"Why's that?" Blaze asked.

"Because The Draught slowed the werewolves down."

"What?" I yelled, jerking upright in my seat.

"Hang on." Bez held up his hand, motioning me to pause. Making me want to kill the bastard. Werewolves and vamps? Jesus, Mary, and Joseph, what the fuck kind of life had my mate been living?

"So why did the vamps kill the Eights?" Bez asked, keeping his eyes on mine.

"Because of The Draught."

Bez frowned. "They took The Draught."

"No, they sniffed it. Drove them mad. The second that container burst, the vamps went all...vampy. They attacked without warning. It was...bloody and loud and...horrible."

Her fear switched to terror, then to revulsion, and finally to a deep and almost crippling pain. That day had scarred her deeply, though she didn't show it. My brave little mate.

"You felt them all die," I said, keeping my voice down, sensing how hard this conversation was becoming for her.

She nodded, her eyes going glassy with the tears she held back. "The rush of spirits, of so many dying so close together, was too much. They swept over me and pulled me with them. I crashed into the land between the living and the dead with barely anything to ground me to this plane and got stuck there." Her eyes dropped to the counter, her voice going softer. "It took Percy a few days to find me, and by then, there was no one left to rescue...except me."

That day...a warehouse baking in the sun...the blood and death...the humans who weren't quite dead but too close to it to save…the way I'd run from the vision of her eyes, empty and flat, staring at me from across the room. *Motherfucker.*

I'd been there. I'd walked in sometime after the fight and bailed. I'd left her alone to suffer through days in that place she went when she appeared dead. I'd completely failed her. And yet she looked up at me with an expression of such understanding in her eyes. Forgiving me. Not blaming me in the least. She was way too good for me, and I'd spend every day of our forever making up for the wrong I'd done.

"Don't," she whispered, shaking her head. "You didn't know, and you thought I was dead. This isn't your fault in any way."

I pulled her stool so she sat between my spread knees. Once settled, I wrapped my arms around her and kissed the top of her head, whispering sorry, needing to apologize whether she saw my faults or not.

"And the werewolves?" Bez asked, interrupting our moment and earning a glare from me for it. "I'm sorry, Jameson, but we're on a tight schedule and need to understand. There's a lot at stake here."

I kissed Aoife's head again, whispering, "Go ahead, beautiful."

"We ran into them outside Phoenix," Aoife said, still cuddled against me. "Total freaks of nature, those things. Rotting as they walk around but not really dead. I thought you guys were the same when we first pulled up to the lighthouse, but the time of day and the size were wrong. Percy and I had never run into shifters before, so we didn't know."

"Werewolves are controlled by the phases of the moon," I said, my lips against her hair. "Shifters choose which form to be in and change at will. Werewolves are overtaken and devoured by the beast within; we're able to balance between the wolf and the human."

"Jameson is correct." Bez nodded. "So you shot a werewolf?"

"I shot three."

The room went quiet and still, four sets of eyes staring at my mate.

"Three," Bez said, his voice disbelieving. "They were together...like in a pack?"

"I don't know if they were in a pack or anything," Aoife replied, glancing at me, no doubt unsure why what she'd said had made all of us tense up. How could she? She probably had no idea what werewolves were usually like. No clue that they never packed, that they killed each other if two happened to be in the same territory.

"But they were together," Blaze said, leaning forward again. His attention completely locked on Aoife.

"Yeah, together." Aoife pursed her lips, an uncomfortable whisper creeping through our bond. "Percy kept seeing this vision of a group of lights in the desert and thought they were aliens, so he convinced me to explore with him. He has a bit of an alien obsession."

"Little fucker," I growled.

Aoife sighed. "Be nice."

Blaze smirked at us, probably having seen similar interactions with mated pairs over the years. "So you shot them with Draught-tipped arrows?"

"Yeah," she shrugged. "They were chasing us."

"What happened when they were shot?" Bez asked, his eyes swirling in that unnatural way they did. Ice blue to silver to gunmetal gray and back.

"They fell down."

"What do you mean, they fell down?" Blaze asked, sitting back, his brow furrowed.

"I shot them, they fell, we ran," Aoife responded, cocking her head.

Blaze glanced at Bez and shook his head. "Werewolves wouldn't just fall because of an arrow."

"Neither would shifters," Gates replied.

Bez growled, long and low. "They trained them."

"Who trained what?" I asked, no longer following the conversation.

"The kidnappers," he replied, glancing at me before focusing on Blaze. "They had a trained werewolf in Louisiana when I found Sariel and Angelita. I didn't think it was possible, but he sat and waited for a command instead of rampaging on a full moon like normal."

"Three in one place," Blaze whispered, frowning. "Aoife, you may have been at their camp."

"Whose camp?" she asked, looking from Blaze to Bez and back.

"The shifters outside," he replied. "They set up holding camps where they kept the kidnapped women. Jameson's team found one a few months back and Bez found another, but we knew there were more simply because more women were missing."

"They kidnapped people?" Aoife asked, sounding horrified.

"Yes," Gates answered, a serious rumble in his voice. "Including my Kaija…twice. That's what you rolled in on at the lighthouse. They'd taken her from our Kalamazoo denhouse, and I was busting my tail to get her back. Again."

Aoife looked him up and down, almost as if taking him in for the first time. "You're kind of a badass."

Gates smirked and shrugged. "So I've heard."

"Everyone fears the Gatekeeper." Blaze chuckled, and then focused back on my mate. "Aoife, if I found you a map of Arizona, do you think you could tell me where in the desert you'd gone after the aliens?"

"Sure, but Percy might know better. He was the one obsessed with landmarks from his visions."

"How about you two go find him?" Blaze said, glancing from Aoife to Bez. "I'd like to send anyone we have out that way to check the area in case they still have a holding facility."

_ her," I said, moving to stand.

_ke to take a few minutes to talk to you, Jameson."

_were hard when they met mine, his statement an
o_ _ot a suggestion. I sat down slowly, not happy to be
separat__ from my mate.

Aoife gripped my shirt and pulled me in a sort of sideways
hug. "I'll be right back."

I kissed her head, worried, already missing her. "Be quick."

As soon as she walked out with Bez, I growled at my leader.
"You didn't trust me."

"No," he said, eyes and voice hard, "I didn't trust her. And
you were under the mating frenzy, which—while perfectly
understandable—means you weren't thinking straight in
regards to her past. I needed to be sure she wasn't involved in
something antishifter."

"Draught-tipped arrows," Gates said, shaking his head and
ignoring my low growl. "I never would have thought of it. So
the drug enters the bloodstream and…what? Knocks them
out?"

"No," I said, remembering the way the wolves fell during
the fight at the campground. "They're awake and alive. They
just…don't get back up."

Gates sighed, shaking his head. "The Draught is meant to
be ingested. I don't think Rebel ever tested it for intravenous
administration."

"I doubt it," I said, sitting back. "It must be an overdose
of sorts. Ingest it and your wolf takes a nap. Inject it and your
wolf goes bye-bye."

"No wolf, no regeneration, no coming back from an arrow
to the heart. Damn, Aoife figured out how to kill us without
even knowing it. Smart girl."

Blaze nodded, eyeing me hard. "I'd like to use her in the
fight, Jameson."

I snarled and slammed my fist on the counter. "Blaze, I

don't—"

"It's not your decision. I'm your president, and I say she will be outside in an advantageous spot when the battle begins."

"I'm her mate," I yelled, my hands shaking with the need to shift, to fight, to defend Aoife. "I should have a say in if she's placed in danger."

Blaze shook his head, his voice calm. "Then you're going to be disappointed."

"Fuck, Blaze—"

"He's here to kill us all, Jameson." Blaze's words, so casually spoken, stopped me in the middle of my thought. "The King could have come on his own. He could have challenged me alone, or brought a small group of witnesses to keep things honest and fair. That's how a true challenge has always been conducted—with honor and respect. He didn't bring a small contingent, though; he brought an army."

His words dropped a lead ball in my gut, making the bile rise in my throat. *He brought an army.* Outside, hundreds of wolves stood waiting, ready to go to war. Inside, we did the same thing. Making plans, strategizing, prepping for a battle to protect our way of life.

Blaze sighed, looking tired and older than I'd ever seen him. "Wolves will die, Jameson."

"Enemy wolves," I responded, my argument sounding weak even to my own ears.

"Wolves nonetheless. They are our brethren, and they will die because they chose the wrong side in this fight. We've managed to get almost two hundred Feral Breed members, Cleaners, Alphas, and pack wolves here who are willing to fight, but there are innocents here as well. Wolves will die, and I want to limit the number of them, especially from our side. I need Aoife and her bow."

"I worry that I won't be able to fight if she's out there," I said, my voice quiet, my weakness exposed. "I won't be able to concentrate on anything other than her. I'll get someone killed."

"You'll fight and do it well, because I'm putting you in front of her. You are her personal guard for the battle; it's your job to keep her safe."

I huffed, feeling both relieved and irritated. "This is why mated wolves shouldn't ride or fight."

Blaze raised an eyebrow. "Mated wolves have a connection to their partner that others don't. You saw Aoife over a year ago, around the time Rebel found his mate, if I remember correctly. You thought your mate was dead, yet you felt her all this time, correct?"

I glanced at Gates, wishing he wasn't around to hear my shameful secret but resigned to answering my leader. "Yes. I thought of her every single day."

"That bond makes you two a tremendous team. Look at Gates and Kaija, fighting side by side. They work well together because they can feel each other. They refuse to let the other down. That's stronger than any other allegiance."

"But it means I put her above my brothers."

"Yes," he said, deadpan. Serious. "You do."

I waited for more, surprise and confusion mounting when nothing came. "That's it?"

"Of course. You put your mate above your brothers, as you should. As we all do. As unmated wolves put certain packmates above others. Tell me, Jameson, if you had to choose for only two of us to walk out of this room, who would it be?"

I sat up slowly, tilting my head. "Excuse me?"

"Me or Gates," he said, so casual and direct. "Who lives? Who dies?"

I froze, knowing how to answer but not wanting to piss off a man I respected. The decision was difficult but not impossible, not with the built-in social structure of our breed.

"You, sir. I'd get you out."

"Exactly." Blaze stood up and moved toward the door. "Your mate will fight with her friend Percy, and your job is to protect them. The witches will be close as well, and I've assigned their mates to guard them along with Cahill."

"Cahill? The Southern Appalachian pack member who's been railing about witches since the first time he ran across Scarlett at the Detroit den?" Gates asked, sounding as shocked as I felt. "He hates the witches more than most shifters."

Blaze grinned as he stopped in the doorway. "Exactly. I think a lesson in teamwork is due to the sheltered shifter. And Jameson?"

"Yes, sir?"

"Think long and hard before you make any decisions about leaving us. There is obviously a need for monitoring out in that desert you love so much. Something you and Aoife could do as a team." He shrugged, moving through the doorway. "Just a thought."

Once Blaze left the kitchen, I sat back, feeling wrung out both mentally and physically. Gates stepped toward the door himself, ready to leave. But I wasn't ready to let him go.

"I don't know how to do this," I said, almost too quiet for him to hear. Too quiet for it to be truth.

He stopped, shoulders tight, his body giving off an anxious vibe. "She's your equal and she wants to fight. You just do."

Swallowing my pride, I voiced the only question I needed to ask a man in his position. "How do you handle it? The fear... how do you deal with knowing she could die?"

He stood stoic and fierce but quiet, giving nothing away. Until...

"I don't. But fighting as an equal is what she wants, and I would never disappoint her by holding her back." He rolled his shoulders and cracked his neck, looking more like a fighter than before, the Gatekeeper back in place. "Being mated to a strong woman means picking your battles, Jameson. She'll be above the fight, you'll be guarding her…this one's easy. Wait until it's her turn to be in the middle of the thing. That's when the urge to grab her, to hide her away from danger, becomes almost unbearable. That's when you'll know what you're made of."

"Has Kaija ever been in the middle of it?"

"Yes." His voice cracked, armor showing a dent or two. "And I hated every fucking second of it."

TEN

Jameson

"JAMESON?"

I didn't growl the second time I heard Sandman's voice through the door that evening. I knew our time alone was up. I'd sensed nightfall hours ago, not long after we'd returned from our failed attempt at having an uninterrupted dinner together.

"Yeah, man. I know." I stared at Aoife as I spoke, refusing to look away from her dark eyes, stunned by how beautiful she was underneath me. I couldn't resist her little smile, so I leaned down for a kiss as I pushed deeper into her pussy. Fuck, she felt good around me, all hot and tight and wet. So perfect. I hated that we needed to leave our den again, that we had to join the others who had assembled inside Merriweather Fields. I hated it with a passion I'd never felt before. But my loyalty still rested with Blaze, and my duty to the Feral Breed and the missing Omegas wasn't over yet, no matter how much Aoife made me want that to be untrue.

When Sandman spoke again, his voice sounded gentler, almost apologetic. "Blaze wants us in the library for a quick meeting in fifteen. He'll send someone else to get you if you're not there."

I snarled low and deep, for her ears only, as our unwanted visitor walked away. Aoife smiled up at me, clutched my arms, squeezed me with her thighs the way she always did when I growled while inside her. So I did it again. My little fairy princess moaned, all debauched and dirty, smelling like sex and me and us together. So fucking perfect in her disarray. I ran a finger down her cheek, whispering, "beautiful" as I shifted my hips faster, worked her toward the end.

"Jameson," Aoife whispered, all breathy and needy. "Please. I'm close, and we have to go."

"I know, beautiful." I thrust harder, hating that I needed to rush, wanting this to last forever.

Sadly, forever wasn't possible right then.

I slid my hand between us to help her along with a thumb to her clit. No way were we stopping without Aoife getting hers. I wouldn't be a man if I let that happen. So I circled and pressed and thrust and whispered every dirty thought in my head, all the things we were going to do together when the fighting was over. All my plans for us when we left this place.

I came with a groan as she did, the two of us clinging to one another through it all. But as I rolled to the side so we could leave our mating bed, reality slammed into me with a handful of words from her.

"You have my bow, right?"

Gut fallen, head spinning, I nodded, hating this. Hating everything about this night, this fight, this crew outside. I wanted to tear them to shreds with my bare hands simply for daring to exist in a world with my mate. I wanted them dead. And I wanted Aoife locked up tight so they couldn't even see her. I wanted her safe.

She smiled, rolling toward me, pressing her lips to mine one last time. I took the kiss deeper, holding her to me, shaking with the need to tuck her in a corner so I could protect her.

"C'mon, dirty boy," she said, the smile on her face something too bright and beautiful for the darkness of the moment. "Let's get cleaned up so we can be on time."

After a quick shower, one where I pouted the entire time for not being able to fuck Aoife against the tiles as I wanted to, we trekked out of the basement. It took longer than it should have, that was for sure. Just leaving the bedroom had been difficult at best. I hadn't wanted to let Aoife out of my arms, let alone my sight. She'd laughed and pushed me off her, but she couldn't hide how much she needed me. Small brushes of our arms while we dressed, constantly moving into the other's space, little kisses and touches as we prepared to leave. She was as desperate to stay together as I was, and if I read her emotions right through our bond, just as afraid of what was about to happen.

"Ready for this?" she asked, looking brave and strong as we reached the staircase leading us back to the group. I lifted her hand to my lips and kissed the back of it. Wishing for more time, more peace, and more of her. Soon, though. We'd make it through the fight, and then I was done. One last job before I retired to spend all my time with her.

Some mated wolves could ride and fight with the Feral Breed, I knew that, especially after my talk with Gates. I doubted I could be one of them.

"I'm following your lead, beautiful. Always."

Her returning grin was everything I needed in life. Aoife held my hand the entire way upstairs and into the crowded library, connecting us physically while I tried my best to keep from throwing her over my shoulder and tossing her pretty ass in the safe room.

"Thank you for joining us," Blaze said when he spotted us in the doorway. "Let's get down to the brass tacks, shall we?"

MATING BITES WERE WONDERFUL things; they were also a total and utter mindfuck to the newly mated.

My body ached at the smallest distance between Aoife and me, the teeth marks she'd given me tingling a constant reminder that she wasn't right beside me. That she was anxious and in danger. As a shifter of the NALB, I was entitled to a Klunzad period. Three days alone with my mate, protected by my brethren. A time to get to know each other emotionally and physically. As soon as we handled these fuckers outside, I was taking my time with her. No matter who tried to get in our way. But first, we needed to survive the next few hours.

The internal struggle continued as the final planning session wound down, the tension becoming something almost physical in the air. It grew stronger when Blaze took Aoife to the side for a discussion with the rest of the secondary offensive team made up of the witches, the Omegas, and her. Offensive...as in she'd be fighting. That thought made me nearly insane with fear. I knew she had the skills to defend herself, but that didn't mean I wanted her to have to.

"Ready for this, brother?" Rebel whispered as we walked into the back hallway.

"Not for a single fucking second," I replied, my shoulders tight, my wolf fur breaking through my skin at points as I struggled to stay in control.

Most of our group were in position, standing in the low light of darkened back hall, mentally preparing for what was to come. What we knew *would* happen: an explosion at the front and an attack at the rear. Blaze had us spread out, covering every way into Merriweather just in case, but the strongest contingent guarded the back entrances. I claimed my spot near a window, watching the darkness outside, trying my damnedest to keep my head on straight as we waited for a sign that we needed to engage.

"Remember," Blaze whispered, pacing the length of the hall

with a slow step. "I will face the King's direct challenge alone. Your job is to protect Merriweather and the innocents within her walls. We must abide by the regulations of the NALB."

His reminder was unnecessary but understood. He had to face a true challenge head on or he'd lose the respect of those who followed him. We couldn't let that happen, but we also couldn't let the attackers give the King an unfair advantage.

Percy and Amber sat on the floor in the middle of the room, hands together and eyes closed. They were deep in their visions, looking for the right moment for us to act, simultaneously searching the future to give us the best chance of success. While our enemies could possibly know about the witch—being that the group that tried to take Kaija again ended up on the property of their coven, it was likely—there was no way they could know about Percy. He was a formidable force and a true jewel in the crown of our strategy.

I cracked my neck and clenched my hands into fists as the tension grew. Even through all the chaotic energy in the room, I could feel Aoife. The mating bites we'd exchanged had given me a sense of her emotions, access to her that I hadn't had before. I felt her power, her confidence, and her fear. Not that the last emotion was unexpected. I'd have bet the farm every shifter in the building was at least a little afraid. Even Bez, normally one of the most stoic men I'd ever met, was rocking on his heels. I understood his anxiety. His mate was in the house but not in a safe room, preferring to share her Omega force with us if need be. She had Kaija and Angelita with her, all guarded by Gates. How anyone talked Bez into letting his mate and the little wolf out of the safe room was beyond me. And yet three Omegas would be better than one, if they could all control their minds enough to be of help. That level of stress was something I could relate to for the first time in my very long life.

Needing to reaffirm her place, I shot a glance to Aoife. My mate stood less than ten feet away from me, bow by her side, shabby old backpack hanging from her shoulder as she stared out the window. Looking like an angel as the moonlight bathed her in a pale, blue light.

"They're here," Percy said calmly, breaking the silence and making the lot of us growl.

"Incoming." Bez pressed a button on his phone alerting the rest of the Cleaners who'd spread out to cover each team around the mansion that the blast to the front was about to happen.

Seconds later, a massive explosion rocked the house, the pressure causing a wind to blow all the way back to us. The sound of settling debris was a dull roar, violent and aggressive in the otherwise silent house, but we didn't worry. The witches had the resulting fire under control. As ordered, not a single person in our group moved from our relatively hidden spots. Instead, we waited. The distraction would come from the front, the attack from the back. Front, then back. Front, then back.

I trained my eyes on that far tree line, refusing to look for Aoife no matter how much my instincts told me to. She was ready, she was armed, and she would make it through this fight. She had her psychic sidekick with her as well, and Percy wouldn't let anything happen to her.

God save his skinny ass if he did.

"Fire contained," Bez whispered, watching his phone. "Azurine and Scarlett are on their way back with their support staff to assist."

Support staff...meaning Phoenix and Shadow. It was the same term Blaze used in relation to Aoife and me. She was to fight...I was to keep her safe. A job that fit with my new instincts as to who was the most valuable player on the field.

I hissed at a movement in the dark, the warning sound for the team. More hisses followed as others indicated they'd seen what I had. Slowly, a line of shifters crept out of the night like shadows coming to life, forming a ring around the back of the property. Probably surrounding the house. But what made me

sick, what finally broke my concentration and forced my eyes
to my mate again, was when three werewolves fully changed
came stalking to the front of the line. Half man, half beast,
completely focused on the hunt on a full-moon night like this
one, the abominations were grotesque to look at. They should
have been decimating the shifters outside and trying to break
in to Merriweather to go after the female shifters, something
they could never resist. And yet they stood, silent and still.
Ready. Fully trained and dosed on The Draught if our theory
was correct.

"Motherfucker," Sandman growled, watching them with
wide eyes. "I didn't believe it could be done."

I grunted my agreement, my eyes on my mate. I assumed
the half-dead creatures would affect her, bring out more of
her…necromancerness. Werewolves were an abomination on
earth, something unnatural and not quite alive. The human
side rotting more every day as the animal within devoured
them. And they'd scared her that night in the desert.

She shivered and wrinkled her nose, even her human senses
certainly able to pick up the scent of rot rolling off the beasts.
But as I watched, she squared her shoulders and raised her chin,
pulling an arrow from her backpack. Ready to fight.

Ready to attack.

"Blasius Zenne," a man yelled, one standing behind three
lines of his soldier shifters. "I have come to claim my place as
the leader of the North American Lycan Brotherhood. I am
the rightful king, the one who killed NALB president Xavier
Alfredson after you refused to challenge him as is expected of
our breed. I am the one who will bring back the honor of being
a Borzohn, who will put the Anbizen in their rightful place,
and who will harness the power of the Omegas as the man on
the throne of the NALB should."

Dante snorted from behind me. "We burned that gaudy
throne the first night we moved in here. Even roasted a few

marshmallows over the flames."

I coughed a laugh, my eyes cutting to Aoife of their own volition. She looked on edge but ready. And so, so small.

"You cannot defeat me," the so-called rightful King yelled. "Even with your haphazardly assembled team of those beneath our Borzohn blood. My team is strong and pure, and we're ready to challenge you and your misfit army."

Six shifters appeared at his side, creeping from the blackness of the forest. Each of them escorted a woman, directing them to a spot behind the lines. The women appeared calm...but almost too calm.

"Fuck me," Shadow hissed, looking over my shoulder.

"Is that..." I started to ask, unsure if my eyes were lying to me. But what made my stomach twist and forced me to swallow back bile was the fact that two of the women were swollen with pregnancy.

"The Omegas," Shadow growled, pressing his face to the glass on my left. I nodded, placing names with each face that I could. Sandman's rough snarl carried across the room, and I knew he recognized the women as well. We'd all been doing our best to find them for months, almost the entire year I'd spent believing Aoife was dead I'd also been obsessing over those women. And suddenly there they stood, a hundred yards away.

Fuck the King and his army and the werewolves in the way; I was bringing those women home.

"Well, this just got more interesting." Sandman moved closer to the windows, looking angrier and more out for blood than I'd ever seen him. But sadly, the so-called King wasn't done spouting off.

"Doesn't he watch superhero movies?" Scarlett asked, coming to stand beside her mate. "Monologuers lose every time."

"Totally," Aoife said, smirking. "No monologues, no capes. That's Superhero 101 right there."

I bit back a laugh, unable to stop it, ignoring Bez's glare as I listened to the King talk too much.

"Your bastard Feral Breed members may have stopped me from collecting the white wolf I wanted so badly, but as you can see, I still have plenty of Omegas to choose from. And they'll work for me if they know what's good for them and their young." He moved as if to turn around, but then stopped and laughed. "Oh, I almost forgot."

A man stepped out of the shadows, his face becoming clear as he moved into the moonlit field. Beast snarled and shifted to his wolf form without a word, lunging for the open door. Luckily Gates was near enough and able to wrestle the big animal to the floor to keep him from busting through the door.

"Aaric Reeves challenges Bastian Martinez de Caballero, also known as the Beast of the Feral Breed, in a battle to the death," the King called, sneering as he said the words. "Aaric has a personal vendetta against the Feral Breed member for breaking apart his union with a human who was carrying his Omega daughter. The only human we could find with the right genetics to consistently provide us Omega children. We have an army to build, so he's come to take back what's his."

Beast's roar shook the glass in the windows. Gates growled as well even as he fought to keep control of his brother. Shadow piled on the brothers, offering his assistance to keep Beast relatively under control. Or as much as he could be when there was a man threatening his family.

"He'll blather for another few minutes as his men get into position. It's a distraction, a way to get us to make mistakes," Percy said, sounding exhausted and much weaker than earlier in the evening. "All you shifters better grab some paw. The war is about to begin."

ELEVEN

Aoife

I FINGERED THE FLETCHING on my arrow, my heart pounding and my skin too tight. The quiet in the house, the tension of the group ready to defend their leader, felt blanket-like. Surrounding me, nearly suffocating me, making me sweat. I wanted to fight already. Instead, I stood listening to the idiot outside talk as his followers spread out around the house. As if he could distract us. Did he think we were too stupid to know what he was doing? Did he think we were unprepared?

"Doesn't he watch superhero movies?" Scarlett asked, rubbing Shadow's arm in a small, almost secretive way, something no one else would have seen based on their position. "Monologuers lose every time."

"Totally," I agreed. "No monologues, no capes. That's Superhero 101 right there."

Jameson made a half-choking, half-laughing sound, something that made me grin. He was so tense, his body tight with nerves, that any sign of the Jameson I knew was a good one. Still, I could feel the reverb of his anxiety through the bond we shared. His stress only increased mine, which made it harder for me to find my calm. The man needed to settle himself.

Growls and roars sounded behind me as a couple of the men reacted to the ridiculous speech the loser on the other side just *had* to spout, but I ignored them. My focus was solid—half on the offensive line outside, half on my man. Exactly where it needed to be. It wasn't until I heard Percy speak that I turned away from the window.

"He'll blather for another few minutes as his men get into position. It's a distraction, a way to get us to make mistakes. All you shifters better grab some paw. The war is about to begin."

I nodded and returned to my watch, staring into the darkness at the line of people wanting us dead. I knew we were a strong group, and Jameson said the majority of our team was well trained, but still I worried. If anything happened to Jameson, I'd be gutted. And if anything happened to Percy, I'd lose my mind. I needed to find my balance so I could focus on taking down the enemy while protecting the two men I loved most in the world.

Amber crept beside me, placing a hand on my shoulder. "You ready for this?"

I shrugged. "As ready as I can be."

The witch watched me, an unexplainable sorrow in her eyes. "Percy's a great guy. I've really enjoyed working with him on the planning for tonight."

"Yeah," I replied, feeling as if there were things she wanted me to know but wasn't saying. "He's the best friend I could have ever asked for."

She nodded, looking away before bringing those green eyes back to hold mine. "When this is all over, you make sure Percy knows there was nothing he could have done."

"What are you talking about?"

"You'll know," she replied, stepping away. "You'll know everything soon, I think."

I blinked as she turned and walked outside, leaving me

baffled and wary. Setting my arrow on the windowsill before I rubbed the fletching off, I turned to ask Percy if he was ready to head out. The sight of a hell of a lot of skin, though, sent my thoughts crashing to a halt. The shifters, at least fifteen men and a handful of women directly in front of me, stood naked as they readied themselves to go wolf. I couldn't look away, too stunned to do anything more than stare.

A surge of jealousy through the bond caught me off guard and broke the spell of hot-shifter-nakedness I'd fallen under. My eyes immediately found Jameson's through the barrage of skin. Knowing the feelings were his. He raised an eyebrow before stalking my way, still fully dressed. I bit my lip as he approached, nearly shivering under his fiery gaze as he took my bow to set it beside me. When there was nothing left between us but too many layers of clothing, he leaned over, pushing my back against the wall. Reminding me of earlier in the day when he'd trapped me in the alcove.

"Don't look," he whispered, his voice rough and growly. "My wolf doesn't like it. If you look at them like you look at me, I'm going to have to get all wolfish and claim my mate again."

I shivered when he nipped my ear, pulling him closer so I could feel more of him. "I'm not seeing a downside here."

He chuckled and shook his head, running his nose along mine. I smiled up at him, gripping his arms, holding tight. But then his eyes darkened and his smile fell.

"I don't want you out there."

My glare was automatic, brought on by the frustration his words caused. "Jameson."

"I know," he sighed and dropped a kiss to my nose, his hands kneading my arms. "I just hate the thought of you being in danger."

"I thought we were past this. I'll be on the porch roof, above the fight. Percy will be helping me and you'll be below, guarding us both."

"I know."

"Then you know that I've got this, and you'll be close enough to help me if I need it. And believe me, I'll be keeping an eye on you as well." I leaned up on the balls of my feet and nipped his bottom lip, trying to hang on to a sense of confidence so he would feel it. "When this is over, I'm going to be really fucking pissed at you for the last-ditch effort to keep me out of the fight."

He growled, squeezing me as he lifted, my toes left barely touching the floor. "When this is over, I'll be thrilled to have you yell at me every single day because it means you're alive."

I melted against him, kissing him soundly. He replied by yanking me even higher, tighter. I hung in his embrace, wishing we were alone, that I could wrap my legs around his waist and let him do what he wanted.

When he finally broke the kiss and placed me back on the ground, I gave him my best fake glare. "No fair, being all suave and perfect when I'm supposed to be pissed off."

His smirk was weak, his worry obvious behind it. "I never claimed to play fair."

He kissed me again, deep and rough, one hand firmly cupping my ass. I bit his lip, surprising him, forcing him to pull back.

"We have to go," I murmured, trying to catch my breath.

"Be careful," he whispered, giving me one last kiss.

I placed my hands on his chest, fisting his shirt and yanking him down to me once more. "I will if you are."

"Always." He nuzzled my neck before pulling back, leaving me leaning against the wall. "I'll be right below you, so don't worry. Just keep shooting."

"Okay."

"Okay." His hands—big, strong hands—grabbed hold of his T-shirt and yanked it over his head. He kept his eyes on mine as he dropped those same hands to his waist, smoothly unfastening his jeans. The tease of it, the fact that I was watching him strip in front of so many others, made my muscles go liquid. I ran my finger along that denim flap, the one giving me a peek of the tip of his dick nestled in the dark blond curls of his happy trail. Not touching…not yet. Wanting to, but knowing we were out of time. When the back of my knuckle ran along the ridge of him, he gave me a quiet growl, one that made my stomach clench with need.

"God, woman, you are such a tease."

"You like it." A quick run of my finger over the tip and I smiled, pulling away, knowing we needed to stay serious and ready.

"I love it." With a wink, he pushed the material down his legs and kicked it off, standing naked in front of me. Naked and hard.

I couldn't joke, couldn't tease or make a sarcastic comment. All I could do was stare, want, crave…and worry.

"Stay alive, okay?" I murmured as his eyes held mine.

He lunged for me, shoving me into the wall as he kissed me with all he had. Tongues swirling, teeth gnashing, we clung to one another urgently. Desperately. But as the kiss shifted gears, he softened his grip, stroking my hair, his touch gentle and loving. And when he finally pulled away, he rested his forehead against mine, breathing hard, shaking.

"I fight for you, Aoife. For us."

"I know."

With one last look, a fiery, needful one, he was gone, transformed into a gray wolf. Huge was the only way to describe him. Huge and scary. I had no idea how anyone who didn't know it was Jameson could see this animal and not piss themselves. But he was still my mate, in the softness of his eyes as he waited for my reaction, in the way he watched me, attentive and caring. The animal Jameson was mine just as e human one.

 his trepidation, I nodded, indicating he should come to me with an outstretched hand. He padded to my side, showcasing the strong, slow gait of a predator hunting prey, and nudged me with his nose. It was such a gentle touch, a sweet little move any domesticated dog would have done as well. So very normal. Trusting him, wanting to touch, I stroked his fur, amazed at how soft it was. How much of human Jameson shone through his blue eyes.

"When this is over," I said, grabbing the ruff of his neck and rubbing to relax him. "I want to sit with you in this form. I want to bask in the sun for a whole day as I get to know your wolf side."

He growled softly as I stood to walk with him outside. I hoped that was his way of saying yes because I really did feel the need to understand both sides of his personality. Just like he'd need to understand both sides of mine—the living me, and the one that danced at the edge of death. The one he'd seen once and run away from.

When we reached the edge of the porch, Jameson and I had to split up. He'd be on the ground, defending the final line before the house while I'd be up above. I liked height to oversee the battle and sight my targets better, so Percy and I climbed on top of the porch roof to get a better overall view. Once in position, I pulled an arrow from my backpack and notched it, not yet drawing the bow, watching the crowd across the field. Ready. Waiting.

The first howl came from the tree line, a harsh, soulful sound fitting the full-moon night perfectly. But then the rest of his friends joined in, creating a chorus. Growing louder with every second. The sound surrounding us. Coming from all sides.

A harsh, groaning death wail joined the noise, the werewolves adding their voices as the man who called himself the King yelled to his team to "go forth and take back what you deserve." I snorted; the only thing they deserved was a solid ass-kicking for daring to attack a man such as Blaze. I hadn't known him long, but he seemed like a wise and caring leader, one who made decisions in the best interest of his followers and not for the sake of money or power. He'd been kind to me, even kinder to Jameson, and for that, I'd fight for him.

The night grew louder, more action and less tension. And while Death definitely danced on the air, I allowed myself to hope that he would remain on the opposite side of the battlefield. That he would claim our enemies and leave Jameson's team intact. Leave my new friends to be blessed with another day.

Still, I knew we were ready. We had a plan, we had an excellent team, and we all had solid reasons to fight to the death. Mine stood just below me, howling with his line, his fur silver in the moonlight. He'd survive. If I had to go after his spirit and drag him back to this plane, if I had to make a deal with the devil himself, no matter what was to come tonight, Jameson would survive. I'd die to make sure of it.

Amber and her sisters stood below us on the porch steps, hands linked, muttering what sounded like a poem. Witches pulling their magic within them. Kaija, a woman named Sariel, wolf-bound Angelita, and a red-haired woman who looked two steps into her grave stood on the porch. Blaze had said they were all Omegas, offering whatever it was their power gave to the pack of wolves ready to defend Merriweather Fields. In all, there were eight women with different strengths and powers, all fighting for the same cause. Fighting for those we cared about. Something the King couldn't have been prepared for. He was ready to fight the men, to think like a lone wolf instead of a mated one, but the women behind the men of the Feral Breed were about to knock him off his imagined throne.

TWELVE

Jameson

THE FIGHT BEGAN AS they do; not with a gunshot or a planned attack, no yelling *charge* or anything you see in movies. Our battle shifted from standoff to full-attack in the blink of an eye. No warning, no preparation. There was a split second of anticipation as our side stood, still and ready, a wall of wolves larger than the one on the other side. One moment, and then we attacked as a single unit, each person stepping off in sync. I don't think our enemies were quite ready for that, nor were they ready for the sheer numbers we'd assembled.

Wolves leaped from windows and rushed out doors, racing across the field. Alphas and their packmates, Feral Breed members, Cleaners…all the men and women who'd responded to our SOS. The lawn filled with our teammates, putting the odds in our favor even up against werewolves and a group with multiple Omegas stoking the fires. Our group had Omegas as well, ones who truly cared for us all and wanted us to win. Their powers would be smaller but stronger than the women being forced to submit, because they fought of their own choice. Kaija, Angelita, Kalie, and Sariel—their support was vital and appreciated.

I held my position between the porch and the fight, a final line of defense. Inching out onto the battlefield, keeping Aoife close enough to monitor even though she was almost a full story up. Guarding her as I moved farther afield, never straying too far. She stood tall and unafraid, a warrior goddess overlooking the battle at her feet, shooting her bow with practiced ease. Percy stayed behind her, whispering directions and targets as he watched things play out ahead of all of us.

As the sounds of the battle intensified, a knot of wolves made it through our front lines. They came at me running, teeth bared and ready to brawl. Cahill, who was guarding the witches under Aoife, raced to my side, the two of us stopping the group in their tracks as we fought and dodged. Teeth bared and claws sharp, I snarled my rage and attacked them with a brutality that almost shocked me. But I had the most important reason to fight behind me. There would be no getting past. Not tonight. Not with my mate out here.

I took on two wolves at once, using the weight of my larger body to keep them off-balance. Cahill did the same, both of us refusing to let the wolves past. But then two more showed up, and two more, and suddenly I looked up to see Cahill too far away to be of any help. They'd herded us apart, creating a gap in our line. Seeing that opening caused me to fight harder, to bark louder in an attempt to warn my mate. She must have understood because, seconds later, one of the wolves attacking me fell, victim to her Draught-tipped arrow.

The battle raged on as I forced the wolves to move where I wanted them, drawing them back to the center. Aoife kept firing, helping Cahill and me when things got too crowded, or whenever she could see an opening. I really had no idea what her battle plan was, but it worked. Slowly, the number of wolves dropped, though they were always replenished. It was a never-ending cycle, but with Aoife helping, one we could keep up on.

On a lunge to ward off a large, red wolf trying to go over me, I slipped, and a dark gray fucker took advantage. The burning pain of teeth tearing the flesh of my hip had me spinning, backing up, switching to the defensive. I tried to keep the three wolves surrounding me in my peripheral vision as I protected my rear, but the one had gotten me good. But not good enough. I limped into the scrum, still growling, refusing to give up.

Aoife's voice screaming my name made my wolf whine, but we stayed focused. I knew from the fear and rage coming through our bond that she'd seen the blood on my flank. If I wanted to keep her safe, though, I had to ignore her. Had to focus on the three wolves still trying to take me down so they didn't get past me. Teeth bared and ready to attack what they saw as a weaker target, they circled, playing with me, waiting for me to slip again. Not that I would.

Already my hip was healing, my body regenerating. I'd been a fighter for longer than most unmated wolves had been alive. There wasn't much that could stop me when I wanted to win. I could have lost that leg and still beaten the three before me. It was a lucky break that the one managed to get ahold of me, but that would be the end of his luck.

All three wolves jumped as one, looking to overpower me. I rolled back as they landed, taking them where I wanted to go. Three-on-one was tough, but I'd beaten more with less of a reason to do it. A subtle whistle from my right told me Bez must have noticed the pileup. I ducked, knowing what was coming. The other wolves, unprepared for a shifter who fought as quietly as Cleaner Beelzebub, lifted their heads, snarling, growling, and baring their teeth. A gold disc sliced through the air. Bez's chakram danced through the night, hitting exactly where it needed to, beheading the wolf at my right as if his neck were made of smoke. That left me with only the two to focus on, and they both seemed a bit stunned. Not surprising—most modern people had never heard of a chakram, let alone seen one thrown with the skill and accuracy that Bez could. These fuckers had no idea what they were dealing with when they showed up on Blaze's doorstep. But we'd teach them.

I dropped to a fighting stance, kicking my back legs, letting them know I was healed up and ready to go. They growled, trying to sound dangerous, but the rumble wasn't nearly as forceful as before. Not quite so vicious. And by the way they hesitated to attack, I assumed the two might have realized they were far outmatched in this fight. Which they were.

Aoife shot an arrow into the one on the left, knocking him over. The poor bastard fell to his side and lay there, eyes wide and panicked even as his breathing slowed. Dying a little bit at a time. I chuffed—my mate had wicked accuracy with that bow of hers. Something the last attacking wolf noticed. He turned to stare at her, growling, looking ready to attack.

My wolf lost his ever-loving mind.

I used the last bastard's moment of distraction to my advantage, jumping on his back before he had time to look away from my mate. My claws ripped through his flesh with ease, my teeth sinking deep into his neck as I powered him to his side. I was a man possessed, determined to remove the threat to my mate. Constantly attacking, never giving him a chance to return blows, forcing him into submission with the sheer consistency of my strikes.

When he finally surrendered to his death, I jumped to my feet and howled my victory. Aoife cheered from her post, blowing me a kiss when I turned her way. Head up, tail high, I pranced a bit for her before checking on Cahill. He fought alongside Sandman as Amber backed the two of them up— wolf, witch, and tiger working together. As I watched, a wolf grabbed Cahill's back leg, trying to flip him, which could have been a death sentence for the shifter. But Amber was quick with some kind of magic that knocked the attacking wolf over and gave Cahill a chance to regain his feet. The irony of a man who hated witches being saved by one was not lost on me.

I edged across the grass toward the center of the field, going slowly and evaluating the fight before me. Even as I analyzed the fighters in the battle, I kept Aoife in my sights. She continued to amaze me, shooting steadily, knocking down wolf after wolf. Levi—one of the other Cleaners—finished off her targets in his human form, scowling as he jumped from one fallen wolf to the next and used his knife to end their suffering that much sooner. He took out a few she hadn't hit as well. The man was definitely racking up kills, and all without shifting.

Bez threw chakrams and beat down wolves with his bare hands. The rest of the Cleaners made up the front line, the ones doing the most damage through the enemy's troops. Feral Breed members and pack Alphas stayed in the middle of the field. Rebel's crew worked on that second line, blocking oncoming wolves and protecting our sides from sneak attacks. Cahill and I guarded the back, doing what needed to be done to help our brethren and keep our wards safe. Shadow and Phoenix were on our line as well, protecting their mates as assigned. Those witches had some major voodoo magic happening on their end of the field, throwing wind and light all over the place like they were in some kind of action movie. And the Merriweather guards, the faceless, nameless strangers I walked past every day, fought all over the field with a ferocity I hadn't expected. Our side was definitely more prepared, better trained, and more accustomed to working as a team than our attackers. A major boon for us. A major blow for our enemy.

Everything seemed to be going smoothly—our team seemingly intact, the fight in our favor—until Aoife dre her bow.

THIRTEEN

Aoife

"LEFT, GRAY ON THE MOVE."

I acted before Percy finished his instructions, shooting a Draught-tipped arrow into the side of the large, gray wolf. He'd been sneaking along the edges, heading straight for a skirmish between four wolves. He would have been unnoticed until it was too late and, therefore, was a good one for me to pick off. The animal fell as expected, though from the way the arrow stuck up in the air, I knew I hadn't hit him quite where I wanted to. Percy did as well.

"You missed."

I huffed. "Maybe an inch from bull's-eye. That's not missing…it's a damn good shot."

The fighting below continued, growls, snarls, and whimpers peppering the night air. I kept my bow up—not drawn, but arrow nocked and at the ready—as I waited for a clear target or for instructions from Percy.

"Wasn't it you who used to say—brown creeper, far that a good shot wasn't good enough?"

"True." I smirked, having hit the brown wolf e I wanted. "But I'm allowed a little flexibility stance."

"Please," Percy laughed, scanning the fight before us. "You're so set in—"

He never finished his sentence. His body went stiff as he slowly turned to the right, looking over a cluster of wolves fighting, eyes wide.

"No." He jumped up, completely focused on something across the field.

His whispered word sent a chill down my spine. "What is it?"

"No!" he yelled, his voice tight and high. I spun, bow up and drawn, but he was gone before I could stop him. He jumped from the porch roof, landing with a roll before racing across the grass. Chasing...someone.

"Percy!" I jerked to follow him, slipping when I tried to spin. My knees hit the roof tiles, the jolt making me drop my bow. Heads turned at the clatter of the bow sliding off the roof, but I ignored them. I scrambled to my feet and jumped down from the porch, chasing after my friend. He moved with an athletic grace I rarely saw from him, dodging bodies both human and canine. Chasing Amber.

I followed him, Scarlett and Azurine quickly joining me in our dash across the grass.

"What're they doing?" Scarlett asked, eyes on her sister. "Amber went all Magic Eight Ball and took off."

"No clue. Percy just screamed and jumped off the roof." I swung wide, changing my path to see what was up ahead. Jameson in wolf form caught up, barking as he cut in front of me. Anger seeped through our bond along with a healthy dose of fear. I'd scared him, and he wasn't happy about it.

"Sorry, but..." I huffed, unable to really speak with how winded I'd become. "Keep...up."

He growled but stayed close to my side. Shadow loped ~ the witches, the lone feline in a sea of canine energy. Not a one of us knowing what the hell was about to happen and why the two psychics were running as if their asses were on fire.

A huge wolf, one that looked to be Phoenix, jumped in front of us, knocking aside a wolf heading our way. I changed direction midstride, avoiding both, pumping my arms and legs as hard as I could to catch up to Percy. Up ahead, two large, black wolves and two white ones battled violently with two werewolves. I knew the black and white wolves to be on our side, Gates and his brother Beast, along with Kaija's father and brother. Our team fought hard, but the werewolves had a range of motion that gave them an advantage. With their long arms, they could knock a wolf out of the way easier, and that meant our guys were suffering from blocks and blows to the head. Still, they fought, obstructing the werewolves' path and not letting them near the shewolves. But what made me gasp, what nearly stopped my heart as the overall scene registered, were the two red enemy wolves sneaking up alongside the fight.

"Amber...don't." Percy's yell attracted the attention of the group, particularly one of the werewolves. He sniffed and grunted, smelling the approaching witches. Staring at them hungrily while still batting around our team. The two red wolves jumped into the middle of the fight, distracting everyone and giving the werewolves the upper hand. I itched for my bow, feeling helpless and at a loss as to what to do. Maybe if I'd stayed on the roof, I could have helped them. I doubted because of the distance, but maybe, and that thought buried me in a mound of guilt. Especially as the tingle of Death settled over me.

"No," I whispered, coming to a stop some forty feet from the fight. I saw it before it happened, could calculate the trajectory of the hit as the werewolf pulled back his arm, claws extended. One black from our side—too busy fighting off a red wolf in the middle of the scrum—his intended target. Gates or Beast...brothers and mated wolves, one with a small baby in the house, the other whose mate was probably watching from the porch. Both needed, wanted, and loved. And there was nothing standing between the one brother and an assured end at the hand of a werewolf.

As the black wolf reared up against the red, the scars running along one side of his face caught in the moonlight, and my heart shattered. Beast, father of baby Ali, was about to die. Death practically danced around him, waiting for that soul, wanting it. The glee within the cold, the desire, told me more than any history of the shifter could have. Death had been wanting him for many years, had been angered when Beast had blocked his plans, had fought hard for his soul on a few occasions…but Death had always lost. Beast was a survivor, a fighter, and he won the challenges Death threw at him. But not this time. Death would have the black wolf. He wouldn't be denied again.

And there was nothing I could do but watch.

But as the werewolf's arm came down, Amber leaped in front of the black wolf, spreading her arms wide and screaming out something about summer. I tried to look away, my eyes burning with tears that were ready to fall, but I couldn't. I wouldn't. Not this time, not with these people. I refused to not bear witness to the end I knew was coming.

The scene seemed to play out in slow motion, every second taking far too long to count. Amber standing brave and strong, blocking the werewolf's blow. Percy reaching for her, scrambling to stop the inevitable. And the black wolf—Beast, brother of Gates, mate of Calla, father of Aliyana—seeing the witch jump in front of him, taking a stumbled step back.

Too little, too late, though. Death had been wanting the witch as well as the wolf, had played with her a few times and blamed her for a soul he lost. Without access to Beast, he relented, willing to take the trade she'd presented him with. Death was ready.

The werewolf struck.

Massive claws sliced through Amber's flesh with ease, her blood spraying the group as she fell backward to the muddy ground. The werewolf roared, hunching over her body, ready to enjoy his kill. Thankfully, the white wolves dove at him, tearing apart the werewolf as three more wolves jumped into the fray to defend our team. Even the black wolves engaged with the enemy again, cutting a wide swath between where the witch had fallen and the opposing line of the fight, going after the enemy with a renewed rage.

Too little, too late for one, though.

Scarlett and Azurine ignored the wolves and the fighting. Their focus was running to their sister, their terror plain on both of their faces. They screamed as they reached her, had been screaming, both falling to their knees in the bloody grass. Hands grasping, pushing, shaking…desperate to save her. To put her back together. Yelling words of corners and elements, begging for something they wouldn't receive.

Death had Amber in his claws.

The glee of the specter, the joy in his bounty, made my stomach turn. For the first time, I understood the loss of those left behind. I felt the grief and the heartache of the remaining sisters. Felt the cavern Amber's death would leave behind in the souls of her sisters. I felt it all.

And so I fell.

It took me ten seconds to be able to breathe again. Another twenty to put my shaking hands on the ground and push myself up. Five more to take that first step. Jameson paced around me the whole time, whimpering and growling, his head constantly on the move, looking for an attack. I couldn't soothe him, though. I couldn't soothe anyone. Amber would be dead in moments. I could feel the end wrapping itself around her, and there was nothing any of us could do to save her. There was nothing I could do to stop it.

But I could help ease her transition.

With a renewed sense of purpose, I rushed to where Amber lay, ignoring the fight that continued across the grassy field. The painful cold hit me hard the closer I ran, the chill of an oncoming death penetrating to my very bones. It didn't stop me. When I reached Amber's side, I dropped to my knees, fingers clutching the grass as the pull of the dead sank its claws in deep. It entranced me, enticed me to its frozen world. Made me want to follow it. But Jameson rubbed against my back, offering the warmth of his body as support. He unknowingly kept me firmly grounded in the here and now. Temporarily, I knew, but didn't tell him. Couldn't. Not until I felt her go, until I knew if I needed to help her.

Azurine cried, pressing her hands over the slashes in her sister's chest, a fog growing around her as her magic seemed to spin out of control. "Why did you do that? They can regenerate, we can't."

Blood seeped through her fingers, the flow unstoppable as Amber's life waned. Shadow, shifted human and naked as the day he was born, worked feverishly to stop the bleeding. Not that it would help. And deep down, I think he knew that.

"I did it, didn't I? I outplayed Death." Amber met my gaze, eyes bloodshot and pupils blown wide. As Shadow cursed, she squeezed her eyes shut, pain a lightning bolt across her face. "Need you, Aoife...stay close."

I nodded, unable to speak. My shaking hands grabbed one of hers, letting her know I was there. That I'd help her. I'd never been near a dying person who understood what I could do for them, but Amber was a different case. She knew exactly what my gift was. And she knew I'd do anything I could to help her.

"Oh, Amber. What did you do?" Scarlett asked, her voice shaky and filled with pain, her fingertips glowing. "No one beats Death."

Beast and Gates crept in behind them, two black wolves

looking on, watching over all of us. Amber saw them and smiled, reaching for Beast. He inched closer, dropping his head, letting her run her fingers over his scarred muzzle.

"I finally got it right." Amber coughed, blood spraying into the air, clutching my hand through it all. Beast stepped back, moving out of the way as Amber gasped and choked. Shadow cursed again, trying his best, his hands steady and sure. A desperate man doing everything he knew how to do to save the life of someone else. But he would fail. And soon.

"Tell them," Amber said, her voice quiet and weak. "When it's all done, tell them what I did."

"I will," I promised, though I still had no idea what I would be telling. She needed that sense of peace, though—the calm she'd receive with my vow to tell her story. Needed it to make a smooth transition from one plane to another. I could feel it, sense it just as I sensed Death embracing her torn body. Death lingered, though, hungry and ready to take her where he wanted to…but on his terms.

So we waited, and we wished for miracles as Shadow tried his damnedest to save the woman he knew had no chance to survive. As we watched her die slowly.

Sometimes, death was a gong—a cacophony of sound and emotion that would pull me under like a tidal wave, overpowering my resistance and desire for life. Not that night, though. The death of the witch named Amber Weaver was silent and calm, a simple passing from one form to another, almost an absorption of the spirit by the earth below us. A fitting end for a woman who so selflessly took the blow meant for another. One second, she was alive, staring at her sisters with a small smile on her face. The next, she lay limp on the ground, eyes empty and heart stopped. Her soul making barely a whisper as it left her body.

"No," Scarlett cried, covering her mouth with her fingers. Shadow hung his head, his bloody hands finally still. Helpless and beaten, he wrapped his body around his mate's as she curled over her knees. And then she began to sob. Phoenix shifted human, his face ashen. He knelt beside Azurine as he whispered in her ear, his muscled arms holding her together. Their tears falling together. A family in mourning.

Interrupted by a snarled warning from my mate.

"You're so weak," a man hissed. Jameson stepped in front of me, his growl fierce as he pushed me back. One of the enemy wolves had shifted as well, standing tall and naked in front of all of us. Threatening in his stance. "You cry over an abomination. Witches and shifters have never mixed, not in the history of our glorious breed, and yet you mourn her."

Beast shifted human, dark fur transforming to brightly painted skin in a breath. Handsome as Gates but with scars and ink decorating his body, he looked like a man about to explode. Like a firecracker gone wrong.

The enemy's eyes lit up in glee, though. "Oh, there you are. Tell me, Beast of the Feral Breed, is my daughter here?"

Beast growled, low and deeply dangerous even to my ears. "Fuck you, Aaric."

Phoenix uncurled from around Azurine, passing her to Shadow and standing to his full height, his growl adding depth to Beast's.

Aaric smirked, not seeing the danger of poking the tattooed man, apparently. "Maybe not. Perhaps her mother, then? My men could use a little entertainment… They do so miss hunting her down and rutting her into the forest floor. I made sure there was no penetration—I couldn't have her spoiled in such a way, of course—but her screams were so delicious. I enjoyed watching them have their fun."

Phoenix jerked forward, shifting to his wolf, snarling and crouching into an attack pose. But Beast stayed human, growling steadily but otherwise appearing calm. Calm and lethal.

"This pup one of your friends, Beast?" Aaric said, chuckling. "Maybe I should call over the rest of my team, teach him a lesson in messing with witches like we did with that other wolf from your den. I think I heard his name was Numbers, right?"

"He's mine," Beast hissed, barely making a sound. Phoenix froze, staring, snarling, every muscle tensed. Ready but waiting, giving Beast the lead.

As more wolves approached from the enemy line, Aaric cocked his head, arrogant and brazen, as if he had nothing to worry about. "When we kill that joke of a president, which will I leave with? My daughter or your mate? I'll let my boys have their fun with both, but one will come home with me. Why don't you choose?"

"You'll leave with neither, because you'll be dead." Beast charged, shifting to his wolf form before I could blink. Aaric's sneer fell and he retreated half a step—barely more than a few inches—but it was all Beast needed to gain the upper hand.

The rest of the guys shifted as well, all diving into the renewed fight. Even Shadow, his orange stripes glowing in the moonlight as he left his mate and her sister to their grief. The wolves attacked...all except for one. Cahill, the wolf from the Southern Appalachian pack who'd been so hard on the witches, stood at Amber's feet. Watching the fight, growling whenever anyone came near. Guarding the witches who'd just lost one of their own.

FOURTEEN

Jameson

I RACED AROUND THE werewolf that had killed Amber, fighting back Aaric's pack with a vengeance born of pure rage. Aoife's emotions fed mine, her fear and sadness stoking the flames of my anger. My mate sat quiet and still behind me, eyes unfocused, air around her almost visibly cold as the emotional connection between us surged with pain. I worried for her, but Percy sat next to her, holding her hand. As much as the little fucker annoyed me, he was her friend. He'd take care of her while I took care of what I needed to. So instead of comforting my mate and panicking that she'd get lost in something I couldn't understand, I sought revenge for the death that had led to her sadness. I fought for justice.

Beast fought as well, looking like…well, a beast. He raged past Aaric's pack like a tornado, diving onto the lead man himself. I understood that single-minded obsession more now than I ever had. Aaric had harmed his mate, threatened his family, and was trying to lay claim to the baby Beast saw as his own. Aaric needed to die, and Beast needed to be the one to take him down.

I focused on helping my team kill the last werewolf, forcing him back and keeping him clear of the shewolves he sought. The thing fought hard, jumping and snapping his jaws, using his height to his advantage, swinging his arms in huge arcs. I fought harder, though—twisting, herding, barking at the animal, using claws to wear him down.

"My turn, Jameson." Levi raced to my side, almost giddy as he jumped at the werewolf while screaming a battle cry. The Cleaner fought with a smile on his face, finishing the unnatural monster off within moments, but not before batting him around like a cat with a toy.

We all knew the moment Beast overtook Aaric by the mighty snarl his wolf gave. The big, black beast jumped on top of the smaller, gray one, sinking his teeth in deep. No preamble, no lead-in, no delay. Simple, clean, and efficient…and exactly what I expected. There was no way Beast would worry about pomp and grandstanding, and there was nothing Aaric could possibly do to fight against a rage like that. Beast wanted that man dead, needed to kill him to keep his family safe. End of discussion.

Growling the entire time, Beast held Aaric down as the smaller wolf bled out. An agonizingly slow and painful death to be sure. Exactly what the asshole deserved.

As the fighting on our end began to peter off, the enemy wolves killed or corralled into holding areas, one big battle was about to begin across the yard. A war that could only be fought one-on-one.

Blaze versus the King.

The King had challenged Blaze directly, meaning Blaze *had* to fight him. If he didn't, almost every shifter in the country would make an attempt for his seat. But if he fought, he had to win. The other alternative was no alternative at all. A true challenge meant a fight to the death.

Aoife came to my side, reeking of death but warm and craving my touch. Thank fuck for that. Her emotions were still a blend of pain and anger, mostly pain, so I knew she was taking the death of Amber hard. Once I shifted human, I pulled her in tight, wanting to hold her, needing to soothe her the only way I could. She curled into my body, wrapping an arm around my back and placing her other hand on my chest. Calming me with *her* touch.

"This is going to be ugly," I whispered just as Blaze and the King faced off.

"I thought we'd already seen ugly today."

Her tired voice made me want to pick her up and carry her back to the basement room we'd spent so much time in already, but I couldn't. There was still so much to do. Including watching to see if our president would survive the night.

The two men circled one another, the King's last guards joining a line of our wolves as we stood back to watch. We would all keep it fair, make sure that the fight remained one-on-one with no weapons and no assistance offered. Only one shifter would be walking away, and he'd do it completely on his own.

Blaze crept counterclockwise, his eyes on the King. Waiting and watchful. The man had more patience than most; he wouldn't make the mistake of jumping the gun. So he allowed the King to make his first move. The air practically vibrated as the two moved in a circle, almost dancing. Every shifter stood silent and respectful, the night quiet as well. It was as if Mother Nature herself knew how important this battle was to the future of our breed. As if she, too, felt the tension.

With a snap, the King shifted, going from two feet to four in a moment. Blaze mirrored him, clothes falling to the ground as the two men raced at one another in wolf form. They met teeth first, growling, snarling, viciously biting and tearing at each other. My mate gasped and tucked her head into my arm, hiding. I couldn't blame her—the fight was brutal and hard to watch, even for someone as seasoned as me.

As the fight continued, the crowd grew louder. Men growled and howled with every hit, both sides cheering for their leader. Strength-wise, the battle was pretty well matched, which led to a long fight full of painful hits and blood. At one point, the King raked Blaze across the muzzle with his claws, spraying blood high into the air. Blaze yelped and jumped back, shaking his head.

"Oh, no," Aoife said, moving as if to step into the circle. I grabbed the back of her shirt and pulled her toward the mansion, using my body to block her view.

"Easy, killer."

She looked up at me, pupils wide, eyes panicked. "Death is near. He's coming back."

I swallowed hard, hoping for Blaze to come out on top, knowing there was always a chance he wouldn't. "True, but we can't pick who lives and who dies."

"What?" Her brows came down, her mouth twisting to a frown. "But he's your leader."

"And to lead a group of wolves, he has to prove himself. He has to be the toughest. If he can't beat his enemy alone, he can't lead."

She paused, watching me. I could almost see all the cogs in her head turning that information over.

"That's barbaric," she said, her words hard.

I shrugged, knowing it but accepting it as well. "That's the life of a shifter."

The back door to the house opened, making me jump and growl as I moved between the newcomer and Aoife. Instead of an enemy, I met the worried eyes of Moira. She paused on the porch, face filled with a fear I understood all too well as she watched the fight going on behind us. One moment, a brief display of just how much this battle scared her, and then she was back to business. Shoulders straight, chin up, eyes hard, she handed me a cloak before moving past us. Some of the people from the safe rooms followed—Calla and the baby, Charlotte and her brother. Angelita met him on the porch steps, padding along beside him like a watchdog. More people followed that I didn't know. All coming to see how this all ended.

"Dress yourselves," Moira called to the crowd. Calla and baby Ali hurried to where Beast stood beside his brother, the little family clinging to one another. Ali grabbed her daddy's beard, pulling him down to her, a move that made Beast grin. Gates took cloaks for him and Kaija, then grabbed two more and headed for where the witches still rested beside their sister, Phoenix and Shadow hovering over them protectively in their human forms. Naked in more ways than one, their emotions plain on their faces. Their loss obvious to the world. Charlotte joined Rebel across the field, tucking her face into his shoulder. Her brother stayed on the porch steps, sitting with Angelita by his side—the two parentless teenagers seemingly having found comfort in each other.

Moira didn't speak again, didn't do more than nod as people took the cloaks from her arms and whispered their thanks. She simply took care of all the naked shifters, probably desperate for something to do other than watch as Blaze and the King continued to fight. When she was finished, Dante joined her, wrapping an arm around her, the two mates looking brave and sure. Of course, that was all a show for the wolves watching them instead of their mate. The shifters who would judge Blaze's strengths by the reaction of the two who spent the most time with him. And right then, their reaction was nothing but quiet confidence. I knew Dante and Moira well, though, and could see the emotions in their eyes from forty paces. They were afraid.

But I wasn't...not really.

I knew Blaze as a leader and a fighter, not as a friend or a lover. The man was ruthless and never gave up, intelligent and strategic. He'd wear down the King with his will alone, never giving his attacker a moment to catch his breath. He'd win out of pure stubbornness not to lose. Dante knew it, but he had an emotional connection to the man that overrode his logic. Moira was too new to have seen this side of Blaze before. She'd learn, though. He would not allow himself to lose.

As I expected, Blaze waited out the King. Fighting hard but reserving his movements enough to have more energy at the end of the battle. Letting the King make all the big runs and attacks. Bloodied, battered, and muddy, the two came together in one last round. Just as loud as before, just as vicious, but the King wasn't nearly as fast as he had been at the start. He faltered, tired and weakening. Blaze surged forward. Ready to end the battle. Ready to show he was the strongest wolf in the land.

It was Blaze who triumphed, Blaze whose teeth tore at the flesh of his adversary. Blaze who stood over the body of the King and howled to the night sky in victory. And it was Blaze who finally shifted human and made one request as his mates rushed to his side.

"Bez, please take the Omegas the King brought to the medical wing so they can contact their packs and get some rest. Their nightmare is over."

The shifters who'd been rooting for Blaze howled for their leader, filling the night with a song of victory. The King's few remaining soldiers knelt in the grass, ready for whatever fate Blaze bestowed on them. Luckily, he was a man focused on justice. He wouldn't kill them for picking the wrong leader. Not unless they deserved it.

I let out a deep breath as the Cleaners quietly escorted the kidnapped Omegas inside the house. A year of my life, the biggest mission I'd ever worked on, seemed to be coming to a close. Sure, we needed to go through our notes on each Omega who had been reported missing and question the King's remaining team to verify there were no more being held against their will, but that would come. The Omegas needed medical attention, and the King's soldiers needed time in a cell to make sure their mouths were good and loose. But other teams would carry that workload. For Shadow, Sandman, and me, there was time for a small break. Or more. I wanted to sleep for a week or just lounge in bed with my mate. I wanted my Klunzad period. I wanted to hole up in my den with Aoife and not come out until we were damn good and ready.

But Aoife had other plans.

She pulled out of my arms and headed across the blood-soaked grass. Toward the witches who sat quiet and still, whose tears had left streaks down their faces. Who did not seem ready to let go.

Aoife the necromancer headed toward death.

FIFTEEN

THE ENERGY AROUND THE fallen witch pulled, moving me without thought or intention. I'd felt that energy before. Her spirit was too unsettled and had entered the land between, the purgatory where they weren't truly at rest but not alive either. The dead craved peace, but many had trouble letting go of their earthly forms enough to find it. I could help with that, and Amber knew it. The strength of the draw to her body, the craving within me to go to the land between, that was all her. She knew I was a necromancer, and she was waiting for me. Calling me. Forcing away the energy of all the other dead shifters on the grass and making me focus solely on her.

"Aoife," Jameson said, concern evident in his voice.

I couldn't look at him, couldn't tear my eyes from Amber's dead body in the grass. From the swirling lights around her that only I could see. From the beauty of the stillness. "Remember when you saw me the first time?"

He froze for a moment as I walked on, the bond between us giving me an inside look at his pain and fear. When he finally spoke, his voice sounded rough, broken.

"You looked dead." He grabbed my arm and spun me to face

him, not harsh but a few notches above gentle. I understood his need to be forceful. I knew where his mind had gone. And if I hadn't, all I'd need to do was look at him. His face, my God, his beautiful face. So filled with fear and anger. With doubt.

"Aoife, please—"

I rose on the balls of my feet to press a small kiss to his lips, knowing he needed physical contact. Understanding his wants. Conscious that what I was about to do would hurt him far more than it would me.

"Don't worry," I whispered. "Don't panic, don't lose hope, and don't try to pull me out. Just…let me go. I'll be back."

"You'll be dead."

I nodded, knowing that was exactly how he'd see it even if that description weren't quite true. "Only for a little while."

"How long?"

I blanched, not sure how I should answer that question. "I don't know. Sometimes it's a few hours."

He watched me, waiting, knowing I was hiding something. "And when it's not just a handful of hours?"

I ducked my head. "It can last…a while."

"How long?" Oh, the growl. The anger in his words. He was losing control, and I was pushing him past it.

"A few days, tops."

He lunged and yanked me closer, pulling me against his chest. "Aoife, no."

"Jameson, I have to." I wrapped myself around him, craving his warmth, needing his touch. "This is what I do… It's what I was put on this earth for. Mediums can talk to the dead, but we necromancers can actually travel with them to the land between. We can *help* them. Let me help Amber find her peace. She earned that. Deserves it."

That argument stopped him, made him pause. And, I hoped, would let him see that I was right. I had to go to her. She needed me.

"I hate this," he snarled, staring down at me with a fierceness that made my heart race.

"I know." I kissed his chest, his collarbone, his neck, and came back around to press my lips over the mating mark I'd given him. He hissed, hands kneading my flesh, holding on and letting go all at once.

Eventually, he sighed and his shoulders fell. "You goddamned well better come back to me."

"I will." One more kiss to the mark joining us, another soft one to his lips, and it was time for me to go. Amber's spirit was restless and impatient, making the necromancer side of me flare bright in my mind. With a grim smile, I pulled away from Jameson, hating to see him so worried.

But as I reached her body, I worried. The energy around Amber was all wrong. Death not truly happy with his conquest. Something wasn't aligning the way it should, and for the first time in a long time, I feared what I was about to drop into.

I settled onto the grass, knees touching Amber's arm. Jameson stood beside me, edgy, an aura of tension wrapping around him from head to toe. Hating this, I knew. The two sisters glanced at us but said nothing, too deep into their grief to pay attention to the outside world. A scene I'd witnessed at least a hundred times before.

Sighing, ready to go, I grabbed a small bag out of my pocket, one I carried with me no matter what. Aged linen, dirty with use. It had once been a shroud of sorts, the final wrapping around a dead woman buried in Arizona at least a hundred years before I was born. A woman Percy and I had discovered was another necromancer. A fitting history considering what the bag held. Swallowing hard, uncomfortable with displaying my trinkets in front of so many people, I took a deep breath and dumped the contents of the bag. All the bits and bobs scattered across the ground, a macabre and, some would say, disgusting collection. Not to me, though. The bones and blood, flesh and hair I carried with me were the tools of my trade, ones I refused to let go of.

"Blood magick," Azurine hissed, inching back. Phoenix growled low, looking from me to the small pile of human remains and back, his arms around his mate. Protecting Azurine as if I would hurt her. Scarlett watched from where she sat, her head resting against Shadow's chest. Her body language and the look on her face telling me she was more open…more accepting.

"Yes, there's some blood." I lifted the vial of thick, red-brown liquid. "Just a drop or two, really. That's all I need. Live is best but I carry some with me just in case."

"In case of what?" Shadow asked, watching me.

"In case I get stuck. Being a necromancer means I can travel to the land between the living and the dead to help souls transition beyond. Making it back can be tricky."

Jameson growled sharply, attracting the attention of the witches for a brief moment. I reached behind me and rubbed his leg, refusing to meet his eyes. I couldn't take it again…seeing the fear there. Not yet, not with the energy swirling in a way I'd never experienced before. If he saw my doubt, my hesitation, he'd carry me off and refuse to let me help. And though I'd kick his ass for it, I couldn't blame him. If the situation were reversed, I'd fight tooth and nail to keep him with me instead of letting him go off into the unknown where he might not be able to make it back. But *I* would, I'd make it back for him because he'd be with me every step of the way.

Once Jameson calmed, going almost silent, I went back to sorting through the scattered contents of my bag. Scarlett leaned forward, showing interest in my collection.

"Are they talismans of some sort?"

I shook my head. "Not really. They're more touchstones for my own process. Bones and bits of dead flesh. Things to help me concentrate on the plane where the dead go in between here and their final resting place. Then I have these."

I nudged the remains aside, turning over other less creepy items. "Sticks and flower petals, grass and a crystal. All things to remind me of this plane, and why I need to come back. Of the things I love so I don't get stuck."

"And all that…stuff…is enough? It'll make it so you can come back?"

"It should be," I said, uncertainty in the words.

Jameson knelt beside me, staring at the ground, not looking at me. "What can I do to help? Please, Aoife. I can't—"

I shushed him, lifting his chin with a finger until he finally met my eyes. The pain there made me want to cry, the fear stoking my own. I hated doing this to him, but it was my job. It was what I was meant to do. Amber needed my help, but I would take every precaution to come back to him.

"You're my soul mate," I whispered. "You and I have the strongest bond the fates created. My draw to you should outweigh any desire to stay on the other side. But, there is something I need from you that would make my transition back easier."

"What's that?"

Looking into Jameson's eyes, I grabbed a small knife from my pocket and held it up. "May I?"

He stared at the blade, understanding washing over his features. And then he held out his hand. "Anything."

"I can't believe we're just going to sit here and watch as she performs blood magick," Azurine said. I bit my lip, worried, wondering if I should send her away so as not to be affected by her negativity.

"Shut up, Zuri," Scarlett replied, sounding almost bored… probably exhausted from the emotions of losing her sister. "The blood bond between mates is sacred, a fact you'd know if you'd ever let your man take a nip at you. Sit down and let her weave her magick, as she let us weave ours all night. She's trying to help Amber."

Azurine sat back, leaning against Phoenix and frowning. I gave her my best understanding smile because, while she was sort of right, she was mostly wrong. That didn't negate her fear of blood magick, but witch magick and necromancer magic were two very different things. Something perhaps she didn't understand.

"What I do isn't like what you do. There're no sides to being a necromancer, no dark energies to resist. I assist the spirits of the dead make their way to where they belong. It's not really magic, per se, but there's something inside of me that allows me to go where the living can't." I grabbed Jameson's hand and turned it over, palm side up. Watching him. Waiting for him to give me the okay. "There are spirits who don't appreciate those of us born with the ability to cross planes. They want our power; they covet it. And they sometimes try to keep us in the land between as a way to access the power we're born with. Holding things I love about this realm, things that show life and joy, helps me find my way back no matter how hard they make it."

Looking into Jameson's eyes, I smiled. He leaned down to nuzzle my nose, whispering a quiet "beautiful" before sitting back on his heels. Nodding to me. Flattening his palm even more.

Praying for a smooth journey, I stared into Jameson's eyes as I pierced his finger. And I made him a promise I intended to honor.

"I'm coming back for you."

I wiped his blood on the palm of my right hand, making a star of sorts. Once complete, I kissed his finger to show him my gratitude. He ran his thumb over my jaw, then his bloody fingertip, spreading a streak of red across my cheek.

"I'm holding you to that," he murmured.

Needing to surrender to the pull, I arranged the rest of

my trinkets so I could reach them easily. Living things to the right, dead to the left. Jameson moved behind me, his hands clutching my hips, his breath on my neck.

"Where?"

"Here." I slid down to lie on the grass, clutching the bones and bits of death in my left hand. Once in a comfortable position, I began to think through the levels of life and death. My left arm began to ache, the sting of Death's cold grip closing around my bicep. Pulling me down. I kept my right arm on Jameson's thigh, needing his touch. But as much as I wanted to stay with Jameson, Amber needed me. This was my time to help her, the only chance I might get. Finding her in the land between was not a guarantee, and time made it all the harder to do. My time was up.

Eyes on Jameson's, my soul open to the letting go that needed to happen to move planes, I worried the dead things in my hands and embraced the need to die. One last whisper from my mate, one last moment of connection as he rubbed more blood on my cheek, before I surrendered.

And then the world fell away.

Jameson

"WHAT THE HELL IS that?" Shadow hissed, breaking the silence. I closed my eyes, fighting back the growl building within me. I knew what *that* was, had been obsessed with it for a year. Had let it raze my heart over and over and over again as I wallowed in hell from it.

Death.

Shadow's wolf senses were picking up the subtle scent of death coming from Aoife, a fetid odor even Amber's dead body had yet to emit. The speed with which the scent came surprised me, but I knew it had to be part of her trance. Or at least I hoped. I kept my eyes on her and my jaw clenched, fighting back the need to shake her, to do something—anything—to bring her back. Aoife looking and smelling dead was to be expected, and I needed to learn to deal with it.

If that was ever even possible.

"She's traveling to the land between, a place where normally only the dead are allowed. She has to basically be dead to get there," Percy whispered as I watched my girl grow pale. Her skin lost some of its warmth, her body heavy with lifelessness. But my blood on her cheek stood out in stark contrast to her ghostly pallor, and that was what would help bring her back. Me. Us.

"She's so pale and still. Is she…really dead?" Scarlett asked, sounding worried.

"Kind of," Percy answered. "She's more in stasis, her body is somewhere between life and death while her mind is all dead."

I snarled, my lip curling at his choice of words. The boy put a hand on my shoulder and leaned down to speak quietly in my ear.

"I'm sorry. I shouldn't have said it like that. So you know, her body is tied to this plane. I have faith that she'll be back, but we need to keep her safe in the meantime. I know you won't want to leave her, though. Just know I'm here to help and support her, too. This could take a long time, okay?"

I nodded, accepting his words even though I knew there was no way I'd leave her still body. No, I'd stay with her, make sure she came back. Keep my body pressed to hers so our bond could be at its strongest. But Percy was right as well… however long she was gone would *seem* longer, feel endless. For both of us. He'd been her best friend for years and been with her through some rough patches in her life. Seeing her dead couldn't possibly be easy on him, unless—

"Do you see her?" The growl in my voice had the others spinning to gape at me, but Percy didn't act surprised.

"Never. Her entire future disappears whenever she trances

like this."

I nodded, heart plummeting, both for him and for me. "That has to be hard for you."

He stared at me, as if surprised I'd take his feelings into account. Swallowing hard, eyes turning a bit bloodshot-looking, he nodded once. "It's terrifying. Every single time."

And then we waited.

Percy sat across from me, giving me space. In fact, everyone seemed to back away, leaving Aoife and me next to Amber's body. Alone. As shifters moved around us, caring for the injured and moving the dead, we waited. Focused on Aoife for hours. As the rest of our team moved on with chores and recovery, Percy and I sat in silence, both watching over the woman we loved: him as family, me as my mate. But our hearts were true and strong, our intentions clear. We'd bring her back, no matter what.

As the night headed toward morning, I held on to my almost-dead mate. I clung to her, kept her safe. And I pleaded.

"Come back to me, baby. I know you have a job to do, but I need you here when you're done."

When her body went cold in my arms, I kissed her forehead, grabbed her right hand, and tilted my head back. Howling was not something most shifters did in their human form, but I couldn't stay silent. Too afraid to shift and break our connection, I simply let my wolf spirit come forward. Fur sprouted on my arms and my muzzle extended enough so my wolf could sing his mourning to the moon above. Others joined in my lonesome song, supporting me, letting me know they'd be there if I needed them to. Sounding like a pack.

So I listened.

And I prayed.

And I howled until there was nothing left to sing.

And I waited…a lot.

SIXTEEN

Aoife

I FOUND MYSELF IN a field of tall, green grass; a verdant sea covering slow rolling hills and stretching to the horizons. Waving in the breeze, whispering secrets to the air, the grass met the prettiest blue sky I'd ever seen. Everything pure—unblemished by roads, people, or buildings—with no signs of life outside of nature. The sun beamed bright and happy, warming my skin like an early morning sunrise over the desert, before the oppressive heat had a chance to take hold. Warm... not cold as I'd expected. As I was used to. As the land between had always been.

Shit, where am I?

"Amber?" I whispered, turning in a slow circle, eyes scanning the vibrant landscape for any signs of Death, of cold and gray...of the usual. "Amber, I'm here for you. Your sisters need closure, and I'm here to find out what you want me to tell them so I can help you achieve peace."

"Of course you are, death speaker."

A woman appeared as if out of the earth itself. Long, dark hair lifted in the breeze, her warm skin tone and almond-shaped eyes familiar in many ways. And when she smiled, when her pink lips turned up, I knew she had to be a Weaver. She looked so much like Azurine, there was no way they weren't related.

"Who are you?" I took a slow step back, not feeling threatened by the beautiful woman but cautious nonetheless. I didn't know where I was or how I'd arrived in this place. And I had no idea how to get back, so I'd keep my guard up. Be prepared. Because I had a man expecting me to make it back to him in one piece.

The woman smiled, staying still, her hands clasped in front of her. Looking as unaggressive as she possibly could.

"I am Ximena Weaver, mother of the triplet witches." Soft, her voice practically bathed me in comfort. The warm sound resonated, relaxing me to her presence, but only for a moment. The memory of a growl sounded in my head, reminding me of what I had to lose.

"I'm looking for someone." I edged to one side, turning my body in case she attacked. Ready. Wary. Keeping Jameson in the front of my mind so I wouldn't get sucked in by her magic. "This isn't the land between, is it?"

"Of course not," Ximena laughed, tinkling, bell-like notes that almost seemed to reverberate through the air. She looked over my shoulder, and I turned to follow her gaze. Across the field, two small girls wearing frilly white dresses played in the grass. "This was my favorite moment of their childhood. Sarah Bishop had thrown a Summer Solstice party, even inviting other covens to celebrate with them. The girls were so pretty in their dresses, and they had so much fun with the other little witchlings there. But the three of them, my girls, never really left each other's sides. They were too bonded to one another, always have been." Her smile fell, her eyes locked on the children. "I expected my Amber to join me when her memory disappeared from my vision."

I waited her out, not wanting to offer up any information that might put me in a bad situation. Not that having fallen into a realm I'd never been in before wasn't already a bad situation. But I didn't want to make it worse. Resisting the urge to trust her, I clenched my right hand into a fist, spreading Jameson's blood across my palm. I'd make it home for him. I had to.

Ximena moved closer to the girls, who grinned and laughed as they ran. I followed at a small distance, my eyes on the motherly witch spirit, the grass tickling my legs all the way up to my thighs.

"Amber is in between realms, death speaker." Ximena sighed, her eyes worried, her face fallen into a subtle frown. "My daughters are true friends to one another, and there is much love between them. But Amber is too attached to her sisters to transition completely, too much of a prize for Death to simply release to us, and too powerful a witch to be kept out of the Summerlands. She's stuck, not quite alive and not quite dead, at least in her own mind."

"I came to help her."

"Yes, you did." Her eyes, sad and fearful, met mine. "I feel your distrust, but I swear, I mean you no harm. You're the only one who can bring her back where she belongs, young Aoife. Your gift of death speak is sorely needed as I cannot enter the realm of the living or the place between. But you can, yes?"

I nodded, slow but sure. I could help Amber, but first I needed to find my way to the land between.

Ximena's smile returned, hope filling her with an inner light once more. "Excellent. Come, death speaker. I will take you to the door."

I followed her through the grass without any indication of where we were headed. There was no goal in sight, nothing to aim for. Just grass, hills, and sunlight. Blessedly warm sunlight. It poured its light on us, warming me all the way down to my bones. I followed Ximena through the field of green, head up, enjoying the warmth as it calmed me. The heat, the feel of the grass caressing my skin, the peace…it all came together to remind me of how it felt to be wrapped in Jameson's arms. Made me miss him.

"You like the heat."

Ximena's words surprised me, but I smiled anyway. "I do. Usually, the plane where the dead linger is cold to me."

"That's because it's an unnatural plane, death speaker. One forged by the souls traveling there instead of by the Goddess." She turned, smiling, her fingers teasing the tips of the grass as she walked backward. "There is no warmth because the Goddess didn't touch it, didn't bless it with her motherly love and spirit. The dead shouldn't remain there, especially not the children of the Goddess, the witches of the world. We are brought to the Summerlands to be reborn and given chance after chance to fill the world with our magick."

"How long do you stay here?"

"It depends." She looked out over the horizon, her eyes unfocused. "I've been here a long time, and will continue to rest here for much longer as I wait for them."

Distracted by the way the sun seemed to dance over the tips of the grass, I didn't immediately put two and two together. "Who are you waiting for?"

"My daughters, of course. I barely got to hold them as babies. I want to have more time with them before I go back out into the world." Her eyes grew brighter, and she smiled. "You'll help me bring Amber over, the oldest of the three. I'll be able to know one now, but I will have to wait for the other two. Azurine and Scarlett have very long lives ahead of them. Joyous, full lives blessed by the Goddess. We made sure of it."

"Made sure of what?" I asked, my head cocked and my mind spinning. No one could guarantee happiness. I'd seen what happened when dreams died along with a mother, a sister, a husband, or a friend.

"Amber and I, we made sure Azurine and Scarlett could live the rest of their lives blessed by the Goddess, their destinies realized and solid. We couldn't work together, of course, but I helped her visions along as much as possible from here."

My mouth went dry. "You helped her play a game with Death."

"I did. I was too worried she wouldn't have succeeded alone." Ximena slowed, eyes unfocused. "Things didn't go exactly as planned. I had hoped to let Amber join her sisters in life, but the outcome is for the best when considering all that is to come. I only hope you can help Amber cross over to where she belongs."

I nodded. "I'll do my best."

"Hopefully, your best is good enough, death speaker," she said, throwing her hands out wide. "It's time to find out."

I jerked to a stop at a door. It appeared out of thin air, hadn't been there a mere second before. One moment nothing, then a solid wood stopping point stood directly in front of me, scarred and battered with age. This was a door that had been through a battle, one that had survived to tell the tale of a hard-fought victory against some sort of foe. One I almost feared. Cold emanated from the space around the door, an icy draft blowing over my skin. Opposite the gentle warmth of the Summerlands, bringing pain and fear into a space of peace. I'd never felt such revulsion for a slab of wood in my life.

"Like you—" Ximena raised her hand and traced over the carvings on the door "—we have our ties to the dead. We do what we can to help them transition. But witches are not death speakers, so we struggle when a path is blocked."

She closed her eyes and gripped the handle, shaking and whispering as the muscles in her arm flexed and twisted.

"Bring her through, death speaker Aoife. Bring her to me so I can hold my daughter again, and so she can find her peace in the Summerlands. Let her come to be reborn so we can spread magick through the world and strive for balance."

A loud thunk sounded from the latch and the door jerked.

Inch by inch, the slab slowly opened, the darkness inside drawing me through. The cold beckoning, letting me know I was in the right place, that the dead would be there. Waiting for me. Trying to keep me.

"Be quick, death speaker. The specter of Death is not happy with my girl and will try to lure you so he can keep her out of the Summerlands. You are not meant to remain in this place, though, just as Amber isn't. Besides, your soul mate waits for you in the realm of the living. You two have much to do yet."

I smiled, thinking about Jameson, missing him. Nodding, unable to turn around and meet her eyes once more, I clenched my right hand, letting my fingers slip through the still-wet blood of my mate. This was what I'd come for, to access the land between and find Amber. I'd succeed; I had to. Because I had something wonderful waiting at home for me.

With fear burning bright in my belly but my mate's blood reminding me of all I had to fight for, I stepped into another plane of existence.

The door disappeared, the warmth of the sun gone from my skin. I stood in a world much like my own, but washed out and gray. Wrong. Scenes shifted, land behind the colorless overlay changing rapidly until a house appeared out of the dark. A large brick structure, with colonial columns and huge trees surrounding the main building, loomed over me. Everything slowed, flashes of light the only thing giving me a sense of time and place as land rushed past. The cold increased, making me shiver. I moved to a place where the dead littered the ground, bodies of the shifters who'd attacked us, but they were not my concern. I knew where I was headed when I saw the covered porch with my bow at the base, knew where I'd find Amber.

Sparks danced high in the air as I floated across the grassy field behind the mansion. The same one I'd run across not so long ago, chasing Percy as he tried to stop the inevitable. But this time the grass was black, the trees an odd silvery color, and the small amount of light a gunmetal gray. No real colors in this world. No warmth either.

My mate sat where I'd expected, wrapped around a void. Blank space between his arms, blackness covering bits of him where that space must have covered his legs. A blank space that was all of what was left of me, at least in this place. It was an odd scene, one I'd never seen before or expected to. But I couldn't concentrate on Jameson or how my body appeared to be missing. Not when the rest of the vision called to me. Not when my eyes drifted to a scene across the grass.

A young woman crouched behind the gray versions of her sisters, all three washed-out but only one wispy. A soul without form. Spirit without body. Someone dead and stuck.

"Amber?" A chill flew down my spine as her eyes met mine, black and shiny against the smoke-like substance that made up her shape.

"I'm not ready to say goodbye, Aoife. I thought I was, but I'm not."

"This isn't the place for you, Amber. You won't find peace here." I stepped closer, inching across the grass, fighting the urge to curl up in a ball from the cold. "There is a better place to go, one filled with warmth. Your mother is waiting for you there."

She moved closer, floating over the ground. "My mother is dead."

And there it was. The disbelief, the refusal to accept. Knowing this could go badly, I worried my right hand to feel the blood of my mate again, and I took a deep breath.

"So are you. The werewolf killed you, Amber."

Death crept from the tree line, darker and deeper than the shadows. Watching us. Waiting. Wanting. Amber trembled, curves of smoke breaking off her body and circling back to join where once her heart had beat a life rhythm all her own. Something red glowed there, something small and thin, burnt through at one end. Something I'd never seen before in another spirit.

"I figured that," she said, her voice a bit staticky. "I just…I wasn't ready. They don't know everything. My sisters need to know, to understand why I did the things I did."

I kept my eyes on the shadow of Death as I moved closer to Amber's spirit. We had very little time to work with. Already, the chill of his thrall burned deep inside of me, teasing me, making me want to stay. But Jameson's blood stayed warm on my skin, reminding me of what I needed to do. Where I needed to end up. And that wasn't here, for me or for Amber.

Concentrating on the witch, refusing to ignore the threat of Death, I pushed. "So tell me what you would have told them."

"What?" Smoke swirls stopped, Amber's soul hanging still in the cold air as she stared. Weightless and frozen.

I nodded, trying my damnedest not to look at my mate's shadowy form across the grass, to keep my focus on the lost soul before me. To give her my full attention so she'd move along in her story. "Tell me, and I'll take the message back to the living."

Tired, sleepy almost, I shook my head and took a deep breath. I knew the feeling was the lull of Death, but I couldn't give in. I'd stay on my feet, my attention on the spirit who needed me. Death would fail today for both of us; he had to.

Amber moved to the side, smoke swirling again, her body becoming more solid as she stared at something dark off to the side. Something human-shaped. Something familiar.

As she stared at Beast.

"He died. The first time I saw Bastian Martinez de Caballero, the man you know simply as Beast, it was a vision of him dead. I knew I had to stop it. His death was coming, had been chasing him for most of his life, and I had to figure out how to finally stop it. Fate is a thread, you see. It's a string leading you down the path of your destiny. But every now and again, that thread gets tangled, knotted at some random point. When that happens, sometimes, just sometimes, you end up on another path. One that isn't quite the same, but still leads you to where you should be…with a few changes."

Her hands worried the shiny red light at her chest. A thread. Frayed and black at one end, but vibrant and bright at the other, ending somewhere inside of her, too deep for me to see.

"He was supposed to be mine." She reached for Beast, letting her hand drop as her smoke danced along where his shoulder would be in another realm. "My thread and his connected once, long before I'd been born into this body, but he cheated Death as a child and the reaper didn't care for that. Death has chased the man called Beast since he escaped his first fate at his mother's side. Our thread unraveled, our connection severed by the change in his destiny, but Death couldn't win. The three sisters who make up the Fates pushed Beast on a new path, one leading to a human named Calla. The woman who gave him a daughter." Smiling, she glanced at me, looking so much more solid for that brief moment. "Babies, the future of their breed and ours. That's what was important, and I saw it, saw many destinies on four different paths at once. I had to make the choice for his future just for him to have one. And I mourned, because his thread connected to another, giving him a soul mate to cherish. But the end of mine still wrapped around him. Leaving me alone, and yet his."

The red within her pulsed as Beast moved through space in his world. He was set on a task of collecting the bodies of our fallen enemies it seemed, his face locked in a stoic expression. Completely oblivious to us watching from the ether. But as Beast lifted and carried bodies off to the woods, Death swirled at the edges of the scene with a cold and violent energy. Livid that it didn't have a soul to feed from just yet. At least not one of the ones he truly wanted.

"Were you jealous?" I asked, needing to keep her talking, to trust me. Wishing we could leave this place immediately. My poor mate sat quiet and still, head down and chin to his chest. His fear was a living, breathing force around him. Yet I felt none of his emotions, and that terrified me. It was too hard to watch him, to know what my absence was costing him, and not be able to send him a little burst of love or affection. But I wasn't done yet. I fiddled with the dead things in my left hand, staying put for a little longer. I had to be sure Amber made it to the Summerlands before I could go to him. I had to stay put… for now.

"Jealous? No, not really. Not how you probably think." Amber's smoky fingers worried the edges of her thread, white and black mixing into an odd, soupy gray-pink tone. "I never knew him as anything except a chance I missed out on. Even the first time I met him, when I actually saw our thread, it wasn't complete the way it should have been had our destinies not gone separate ways. There was no pull to him romantically. I was more jealous of my sisters finding their own fated happy endings, knowing mine was unattainable. But I had to help them make those threaded connections, to find their soul mates. Beast's destiny was vital to their happiness."

"Beast's?" I looked over the darkened landscape, taking in all the wolves and men walking the grounds. Feeling the chill of eyes watching me. Hungry eyes. The eyes of Death, hoping to lure me to his lair. "I don't understand the connection between Beast and your sisters."

Amber floated toward Azurine, looking over her. Smiling. "His fate is tied to Calla's, and her daughter's is tied to my family's. Our lives are to be interwoven for generations, tied together through love and fate in all the best ways. But him staying alive was the key, has always been the key. Even before I'd been born to this life, the future of the Weavers balanced on his shoulders. It took me months to figure out what needed to be done so the Weavers would go on, and longer to work out how to do it.

"To do what, though? Amber, what did you do?" The world shimmered for a moment, the chill of Death coming closer. I glanced to where Jameson sat, using him as a reference point. Reminding me not to relax, not to rest, not to fall into the trap of the land between.

Amber flew apart before becoming more solid again, more real, with a glint of pride in her dark eyes. "Fates are threads, Aoife. Bits of destiny tied together over time and distance. Events, moments, inconsequential decisions that add up to one long strand of life. But it's a delicate balance to keep all those tiny strands of nothing spinning in the right direction through time. A single event that alters or severs those connections creates a shift in hundreds of others."

"The butterfly effect," I whispered, contemplating all the ways one incident could change a life. One decision. All the ways Jameson and I could have missed each other, could have been kept apart for much longer than the last year. "That's... almost incomprehensible."

"Exactly. If Beast had died along with his mother, Phoenix wouldn't have survived his adolescence, as Beast was the one to take him in, to change him into a shifter, and to introduce him to the Feral Breed. Phoenix found Zuri while on Feral Breed duties and with Beast at his side. The union of my sister and a wolf shifter sparked our banishment from the coven, which resulted in us moving to Detroit where we lived with Beast. That move brought Scarlett and Shadow together. But again, if Gates hadn't taken Shadow under his wing and mentored him, Shadow wouldn't carry as much guilt about Kaija's kidnapping as he does. Guilt is a powerful motivator for both men. Beast felt guilty for the death of his mother and compensated by taking in a lost young man in his time of need. Shadow feels guilty for causing his mentor, a man he sees as family, a pain so deep it practically scarred the earth, so he threw himself into the investigation of the missing Omegas to discover and eliminate the threat still hanging over Kaija's head. Without that guilt, he wouldn't have been fighting so hard to find the missing shewolves. He wouldn't have been in the right place mentally to meet Scarlett, who wanted nothing to do with him at first. Those two would have tiptoed around each other until one of them exploded and destroyed what is to be one of the strongest loves you'll ever witness. The unraveling of my thread led to the strengthening of theirs. And so I pushed them all."

"You danced with Death," I whispered, my eyes wide, my heart pounding. Such a dangerous game to play, for Death never lost. Not really.

"A few times." She shrugged, moving through the air to stand in front of me. "I've been manipulating the future based on my visions for almost two years now. From distancing myself from my sisters so they would feel even more abandoned by the coven that raised us, to pushing Scarlett to accept Shadow. My sisters deserved love and happiness, and I was going to make sure they got it. I messed up a time or two—almost killing Phoenix was probably the worst mistake I made, though the way I pushed Beast to find Calla ranks right up there on my list of "what the hell was I thinking?" But the ends justified the means. Death wanted Beast, but his death would shatter the futures of both my sisters. So I had to make sure he stayed alive, no matter what that cost me personally."

I shivered as the cold increased, Death moving closer, circling us. Ready for Amber, wanting to snatch me as well. "Your bill came due."

"Yes, it did," she said sadly, and then she smiled. "But I win in the end. He wanted Bastian, but I'd screwed with him enough to make him want me almost as much. So when I saw Death making another play for my former red thread, I offered up a trade—my life for Bastian's. And Death took it.

My sacrifice gives my sisters their mates and means the magick within the Weaver line will go on for another generation."

"With Azurine's baby."

"Yes, my nephew." She sighed, smoky wisps dancing along the place where Azurine had sat, a shadow of a memory in her place. "She's so worried about the baby, how the witch and wolf will come together. Will you tell her it'll be okay? Not yet, but after the birth. Tell her I said he's the first of his kind, but that doesn't mean anything at all. Love him, raise him in the magick and the wolf. He's going to be powerful and bring peace to those around him. And he's going to be the handsomest little man who ever walked the earth. A male Weaver is coming, but he's not to be feared. I've seen so much of his future, and he's amazing. Don't let her worry about him for a single day once he arrives."

"I'll tell her. I promise you." I shivered, the cold growing unbearable. If Amber didn't leave for the Summerlands soon, I wasn't sure she'd be able to. It was time for her to go, to escape Death one last time, and head for the Summerlands to be reborn. And it was time for me to return to my mate.

"Amber—"

"Tell them all, okay?" she said quickly, glancing around as if she felt Death slipping closer, knew he was hunting her. "Beast...I don't think he's ever forgiven me for that night on his couch, but I had to get him to Calla. I forced my way into his memories and violated his trust. I'm really sorry for that, but there was no other way that I could see to make him go in time. He's the only one strong enough to protect baby Aliyana. She's the first Omega born to a human mother—their breed is going to go crazy over that fact—and he's the only one who can keep the vultures like Aaric from coming after Calla, which is why the Fates directed him down that path. The mother is important, but the babies are key."

"I'll tell them." A warmth at my back had me turning. The

door to the Summerlands appeared once more, green and blue, brightness peeking through as the scarred slab of wood slowly inched open. "She's there, you know."

Amber looked over my shoulder, both excited and scared. "Who?"

"Your mom. She's waiting for you in the Summerlands. This is your last chance to escape Death so you can be reborn."

Amber's spirit moved as if to pass me, sort of floating across the ground, becoming more solid with every step. But before she reached the door, she stopped, a confused expression on her face. "My mother died soon after we were born. How will I know her?"

I laughed, keeping my eye on the shadows creeping closer, the veils of Death coming to block Amber from her final escape. "You'll recognize her. Trust me; I barely know you or your sisters and I knew who she was right away. But you have to leave now, Amber. Death doesn't want to let you go."

"I know, I just—"

"Come home, Amber Jane." Ximena's voice drew Amber's soul to the door in a way nothing else could have, the smoke pulled toward the wood slab and the warmth emanating from within.

"Bye, Amber," I said, thankful that she'd find the start to her new life with Ximena. "Rest in peace."

Amber smiled at me one last time, fully human again as she stood in the grass of the Summerlands, looking fresh and young and gorgeous in the sun. "Oh, and tell Azurine she'd better get used to hanging out with Beast and Calla. The babies are going to demand it."

"The babies will?"

She laughed as Ximena joined her, the two practically radiating happiness. "They're mates, you see. An Omega wolf shifter and a Mage wolf shifter. Both too powerful for anyone else, so the Fates joined them together. And they're going to know it from the first time they meet."

I laughed, shaking my head. "Babies demanding to be together. Got it; I'll tell them."

As the door began to close, Amber grabbed it, staring at me with unfocused eyes. "Let him help you."

"Who?"

"Jameson. Let him help you with the dead." She traced something in the air, watching her fingers, her voice oddly hollow. "The earth energy of his wolf spirit will make crossing planes smoother and hearing the voices of the lost souls easier, death speaker. Let his wolf help you." She shook her head, refocusing on me, blinking a few times before giving me a small smile. "And please tell Percy to find a shifter named Wilson. Your friend's future is tied to a mated pair on the run. Kalie, Gideon's mate from the Southern Appalachian pack, will help him."

I grinned, stepping away from the door, ready to run back to the land of the living. Death was too close, too spiteful. It was time for me to leave this place before he tried to keep me. "Is that it, Miss Psychic?"

She shrugged, her face serious. "Tell them all I'll miss them and that I love them. Tell my sisters to forgive the coven and embrace their magick. And tell Blaze it's not time yet, but he'll know when it is. His surrender will be voluntary and done in peace; no war can knock him out of his seat."

The door began to close again, Amber and Ximena waving from the sunlit space beyond.

"Goodbye, Amber," I called, sad to see her go but truly happy for her as well. The Summerlands was the right place for her soul, not the land between. And not a true death, either. She'd get another chance at life, a shot at finding her red thread. And I truly hoped she did.

Death blew in, creating a mist that covered the ground around me. Furious and violent, the energy swirled, creating tiny tornadoes that sent smoky wisps scattering. Too late, though, for Amber. She was past the door, in the realm where she belonged. Out of his reach.

As Death's frustration began to tear apart the scene before me, I turned for the mansion, worrying my right hand, wanting to go home. Praying, whispering my wants, calling for Jameson. A rumble shaking the air of the plane made me smile, reminding me of his growl, so I followed the sound. The cold began to withdraw as I walked, the shadows lightening. I could almost hear Jameson, could sense him pulling me, drawing me home. My place was by his side, and that was where I wanted to be. Forever.

"C'mon, beautiful. You can do this. You can make it back to me."

But one final whisper had to be said by the departing witch, one last instruction before the land between disappeared in a whirlwind of smoke and mist. Before I rejoined my mate.

"Tell Scarlett I was the one who set the porch on fire."

SEVENTEEN

Jameson

"C'MON, AOIFE," I WHISPERED, curling over her limp body, protecting her. Clinging to what I had left. "Finish with Amber and hurry back to me."

Pulling her closer, I fought back my wolf's need to whine. My mate smelled of death, her body cold and unresponsive in my arms. I'd expected that…been ready for it. What I hadn't been ready for, and what threw my wolf into an absolute panic, was the total disconnection.

Our mating bond was gone.

"I've only had you for a few hours, beautiful. That's not enough time."

The loss of our bond hadn't happened at first, not as I sat and howled with my brothers or curled my body around hers to wait out this hell. No, the loss of our connection was something gradual. It crept over us, darkening that space where she and I were joined. Until suddenly, without feeling the end, our bond wasn't there anymore. No emotions, no sense of place. Nothing.

I felt as if I'd lost my mate.

"You okay over there, man?" Percy asked for about the fifteenth time.

I grunted my response, wanting to be alone. But I didn't growl at the kid. His voice sounded almost as bad as I felt. As filled with worry and pain. Percy didn't like seeing Aoife this way any more than I did, but he stayed to make sure she came back. He stayed to suffer with me.

"I was an idiot for leaving you in that warehouse. Come back so I can make it up to you, so I can show you how good of a mate I'll be to you."

My arms trembled as I fought back the howl building in my chest. Fuck, I'd only just found her. Or rather, she'd found me. Something I would happily remind her of for the rest of our lives if she let me. If we got the chance. If she'd just come back.

"C'mon, beautiful. You can do this. You can make it back to me."

Without warning, without any kind of sign of what was coming, Aoife gasped and jerked in my arms right as the full power of our mating bond flooded me. I felt her pain and her fear, her pride in having done her job helping Amber. But mostly, I felt her love for me. Hot and bright, lighting up the place inside that had gone dark, her heart and mine reconnected.

"Jameson," she coughed, barely more than a whisper. I uncurled and swept her up my body, practically tossing her into my lap. She grasped my shoulders, shivering, clinging to me like a lifeline, wrapping herself around me and holding on tight. Not that I was much better. My arms felt like steel bands around her, holding her against me, refusing to allow even a millimeter of space to come between us. Refusing to let go.

"Are you okay, beautiful?" I asked, my voice harsh, unable to put into words all the emotions inside of me. But Aoife knew. She felt them. There was an echo in the bond that hadn't been there before, something quiet but obvious. A double dose of the bond we shared. I felt her emotions clearly, but I also felt what she was experiencing from me. She sent all the happiness and relief, all the love even, back to me. A virtual hurricane of feelings blowing. And it was exactly what we both needed.

"You pulled me through," she whispered as she nuzzled my neck, her entire body trembling.

"God, I was so scared." I ran my hands up and down her back, pressing her to me, trying to calm her. "You're shaking, beautiful. What can I do?"

She didn't answer, pulling me closer instead of using words to tell me what she wanted. So I did, I wrapped my arms back around her and pulled her in tight. I even lifted my knees to cradle her as much as I could with my legs. Fuck, I wanted her in my bed, naked and safe with me, where I could make sure every inch of her was okay then wrap my entire body around her. She needed it…and so did I.

Percy placed a hand on my arm. His other hand met mine where it was spread around Aoife's shoulder, slipping something under my fingers.

"Warm and sweet, remember?"

I moved just enough so I could see what he'd given me. A candy bar—simple, plain, sweet chocolate. He'd taken care of her even though he knew it was my turn. He wouldn't let me fail. I twisted toward him, but he was already gone, walking toward the house with his shoulders slumped and his gait slow.

"Hey, Percy," I hollered. Aoife didn't move, but her friend turned, looking over at us with his eyebrows raised. "Thank you for staying with me, and for taking care of Aoife."

He smiled and gave me a shrug too forced to be casual. "I'm the bestie…but it's your turn now. Sweet and warm, always, when she comes back. She'll let you know when she's ready for the sweet part. It'll be a few minutes before she's able to talk or move or do much more than just be alive."

I nodded, thankful, and clutched Aoife to me to keep her warm. Percy smiled and continued his trek back to the house, picking up her bow and backpack as he reached the porch. Taking care of her things so I could take care of her. Letting go in a way. Meanwhile, I was holding on tight. Just beginning to know the woman he'd spent most of his life with.

Several minutes passed before Aoife began to stir. Several more before I finally heard her voice, rough and exhausted but still perfect.

"Jameson?"

I sighed, squeezing her, dropping my head to nuzzle into her neck. To place a kiss there. "Yeah, beautiful?"

"How long was I gone?"

I swallowed hard, my voice rough when I answered. Knowing this was on the short side, that other trips would be longer. That this was an easy one. Because it hadn't been easy. Not for me, not for Percy, and by the way she sounded, not for her.

"Three hours, Aoife. The three longest hours of my life."

"MAY THE BLESSED SUNLIGHT shine on you, Amber Jane Weaver, so that others may come and warm themselves beside your spirit."

The High Priestess of the Parity Lake Coven stood under a tree at the far edge of the property, her hands in the air and her head up. Her voice boomed over the crowd assembled, all of us there to honor a witch, a natural enemy, who'd given her life to protect one of our own. Blaze, Moira, and Dante stood to one side, heads bowed, all three dressed in white to show their respect for the faith of the witches. To show their easy acceptance. The Weaver sisters and their mates stood on the other side, the women crying silently as they let their former leader usher their sister's body home to her final resting spot. A place of honor within Merriweather Fields. A graveyard of warriors lost in battle.

"And may light shine from your inner soul, may the thread of your destiny glow for all to see, like a candle set in the window of a house, bidding the wanderer to come in out of the storm."

The witches had arrived from Michigan while I'd suffered through Aoife's trance-state. Azurine had called them, breaking months of silence between the two groups. Though she'd been banished by the coven, Azurine had felt a full Wiccan burial was needed for her sister, and for that, they required more people. More witches, and the shifters who'd fought for Blaze hadn't balked for even a second. Witches dotted the crowd of attendees, everyone dressed in white as was their custom. They had informed us it was a cleansing color, one of good spirit and peace. Shifters, humans, and witches alike had donned white cloaks and lined up under the trees at dawn. A time for new beginnings and letting go of the darkness. A time for a funeral.

"And may the blessing of the element of earth be with you, soft under your feet as you pass through to the Summerlands, and may it rest easy over you when you are returned to it. The beginning of all life, and the resting place of our physical forms."

I clung to Aoife's hand as the sun peeked over the treetops, afraid to let her go. The funeral, the loss and grief on display, was hitting me harder than the death of someone I barely knew should have. While I always respected the loss of a life, especially in defending our breed, this one hit closer to home. Because of Shadow and his link to her, but mostly, because of Aoife.

Those hours when my mate had been silent and still—when she'd been so near death I couldn't hear her breath or heartbeat—had been torturous. The few hours that passed since she returned, gasping and grasping at me as if I'd pulled her from drowning, had been almost as bad. Aoife had needed to speak with the remaining sisters and their mates, to explain what happened and let them know Amber's soul was safe at home where she belonged. They'd brought in Beast and Calla as well, discussing Amber's acts over the past year, her deceits, and her reasoning behind it all. Aoife filled them in on Amber's bravery, her cunning, and in the end, her peace. How she'd twisted the future to make sure the mates all found their partners and were safe before sacrificing herself so their families could live on.

How it had been Amber who'd burned a porch as a child, something that had been blamed on Scarlett and become a running family joke.

"I knew it," Scarlett had said, smiling through the tears. "I even told Shadow on our first date how I thought it was her. She was the only one—" she'd choked a bit, turning into Shadow's arms "—she was the only witch strong enough to have pulled it off."

We'd left soon after that, leaving the family to their grief. And though Aoife had seemed very open about the tale she'd told them, I could tell she was holding something back.

"What aren't you telling them?" I had asked as we'd headed to the lawn before the funeral.

She shrugged, looking absolutely exhausted as I helped her into a cloak of white. "They know what she did, they know most of the reasons why, but some things shouldn't be told until later. There are blessings to come, but it's not time for that truth yet. I'm a death speaker, but I'm also a secret keeper. And Amber has a few secrets left to tell."

And so we'd walked to the funeral in silence, both leaning into the other. My inner wolf had fought against my human hold through the morning, putting me on edge every minute. He wanted to claim our mate again, to strip her naked and wrap himself around her. He'd seen her as dead, our connections as mates severed. And though the human side had understood that she'd be back—mostly understood—the wolf side hadn't. He had mourned her, truly grieved for her, and he needed a time of reconnection. Hell, we both did.

Needy and craving her touch, I wrapped an arm around

her shoulders and pulled her closer. She snuggled into my side, seeming to understand my needs. Perhaps mirroring them. Likely just as needy and craving touch as I was.

"May the sunlight lead you home, and may the earth rest so lightly over you that your soul be out from under it quickly; up and off and on its way to the Summerlands."

As the wind whistled through the trees, Cahill of the Southern Appalachian pack gently lifted and carried the shrouded body to the gravesite, his face serious. A man on a mission. He'd fought beside Amber and the other witches, had seen them defend his breed, and had guarded Amber's body after she'd sacrificed herself for Beast. He'd obviously gotten past his prejudice and ingrained fear of their power to accept the sisters as allies. And he would bury a fallen comrade with the dignity she deserved. In fact, he'd volunteered.

"May the Goddess bless you, and bless you kindly. May the elements speed your journey to your true home, and may your next life be filled with magick to strengthen you, love to teach you, and destiny to lead you. We return you to earth, dear child. So mote it be."

The crowd uttered a soft "so mote it be" in response. A witch's statement coming from a pack of shifters. A group who wouldn't have gone anywhere near the magic makers before the fight the night before. Leaders and lowly guards alike, showing their respect to a group their instincts told them to fear. It was a moment filled with such a sense of family, I would probably never see another like it.

"Blessings to our fallen sister," Blaze said, his voice loud and strong. "The coven has requested the remainder of the burial to be private, so if the shifters and humans could move into the residence, we'll have a small gathering there to finish paying our respects."

The crowd broke silently, shifters turning to head one direction and witches moving toward the gravesite. Heads were nodded and quiet greetings exchanged as the two groups passed each other. Something again I'd never imagined I'd see.

With Aoife under my arm, we meandered back to the mansion. Cahill shifted to his wolf form and waited a respectable distance from the gravesite. He would perform an act of the utmost respect in a shifter pack, the guarding of the tomb for the first twenty-four hours. Usually reserved for human mates, respected leaders, and elders of the pack, the monitoring was a sign of his acceptance of Amber and the witches into his pack, his family. Once the witches were done with their private ceremony, he would lie in wolf form at the foot of Amber's grave for a full day. Awake, not moving. Simply being there to make sure the body returned to the earth. To show how much he honored her.

I nodded as I passed his wolf form. He chuffed and placed his head on his paws, watching the witches across the grass. Focused. Killian came out of the house and shifted to join Cahill in his wait, an Alpha guarding his pack member who was guarding the grave of a witch. A true first in our community.

"We should rest instead of joining the others," I whispered to Aoife, eyeing the crowd as people passed us. My wolf was becoming harder to control. He didn't like so many strangers around his mate, and he really didn't like that she looked so tired. He wanted her strong and healthy, not worn down and in need of sleep. He was desperate to get her into his den so he could guard her as she rested.

Aoife nodded, unaware of the battle raging within me, snuggling deeper into my side. "Yeah. I need some downtime."

Before I could shuttle my girl inside, though, Azurine yelled for her.

"Aoife, wait." The pregnant witch hurried over, Phoenix following close behind. "I just wanted to say thank you again for letting us know Amber made it to the Summerlands."

Aoife fisted the back of my shirt, as if trying to tell me

something. "You're welcome, Azurine. I hope you and your sister can find peace knowing she's in a safe place and with family."

Azurine bit her lip and gave Aoife an almost shy look. "Yeah, about that. I know you told us what happened and what she said. But did…did she say anything about…"

She trailed off, but by the way her hands dropped to her pregnant stomach, even I understood what she was asking about. And apparently, so did my mate.

Aoife smiled and leaned forward, dropping her voice. "Some things are not meant to be known quite yet, but you have nothing to worry about."

Azurine sighed, relief clear as day on her face. "Okay. Thanks. I just…I stress about a lot of things with the baby."

Phoenix wrapped his arm around his mate and smiled down at her. "I told you to relax."

"I can't help myself." Azurine shrugged. "The past year has been such a whirlwind, so much loss and grief in such a short time. I don't know if I could handle another blow."

Aoife fought a yawn, practically weaving as she stood, still clutching my shirt. Too tired to stay on her feet any longer. At least in my opinion.

"I'm sure Aoife will be happy to go over her experience again," I said, stepping just far enough in front of my mate to block her from Azurine. "But right now, she's exhausted and needs to rest."

Phoenix met my gaze, nodding once as he grabbed Azurine by the bicep and gently tugged her back. "Understood. We'll catch up with you guys later."

Azurine followed her mate as I turned and led Aoife toward the house.

"Thanks," Aoife whispered. "I didn't think I could go over it one more time. Not yet. I need a break from the dead for a little bit."

"Hmmm." I wrapped my arms around her hips and lifted her off her feet, nuzzling her jaw, kissing a path to her ear. "Time for rest."

"Soon," she said with a chuckle, throwing her arms around my neck. "First, I need a bath. I feel dirty."

I ran my hands over her hips, grabbing her ass, pulling her tighter against my hard cock. Intentionally, but not expecting anything, showing her how much I desired her, dirty or clean, but not pushing for more than contact.

"I like the idea of you dirty, but I think I'd love to see you naked in my tub."

Aoife laughed, a sound I wanted to hear over and over again. "A bath it is, then. I'll even let you wash my back."

I growled low, licking a trail up her neck and biting her jaw. Before she could do much more than sigh, I picked her up and tossed her over my shoulder. She giggled the whole way through the house as I carried her ass over end to my room in the basement. To our little den.

EIGHTEEN

Aoife

JAMESON HEADED INTO THE bathroom and turned on the taps as soon as we made it back to his room. I knew that seeing me as dead again would bother him, but the energy he threw off was more edgy and erratic than I'd expected. He was completely keyed up, and I needed to settle him down.

"I don't have any bubble stuff," he called through the open door, his voice harsh, irritated.

"I don't need bubbles." I stripped off my clothes, too tired to fold them, leaving them in a pile instead. They reeked of death, of cold. I didn't want them anywhere near me or my mate at the moment. I couldn't imagine constantly smelling my death would help Jameson relax in any way.

"My soap is just…soap. It doesn't smell pretty or anything."

I held back a chuckle at his obvious annoyance over his lack of proper female-marketed bathing supplies.

"I just need to get clean. Smelly soaps are overrated."

I had just finished stripping when Jameson walked out of the bathroom, wiping his hands on a towel.

"I made the water a little hot, but I figured after—"

He stopped when he saw me, his eyes traveling the entire

length of my body before locking somewhere south of my neck.

"You figured after…" I prompted, but he still didn't answer. He stood and stared, a fire in his eyes that made my knees weak.

"Jameson," I whispered, needing to touch him, feel him, bury my soul in the warmth of his. Needing something only he could give me.

He didn't speak, simply stalked to me and wrapped his big arms around my waist. In a single move, he pulled me off my feet, pressing my body against his as he claimed my mouth in a brutal kiss. Teeth hit, tongues clashed, and breathing was forgotten as we attacked one another. As we reconnected.

I wrapped my legs around his waist, desperate to be closer, to feel more. He held me up and carried me across the room, his hands on my ass, his cock nestled where I was already wet and wanting. But I hadn't been exaggerating when I'd said I was dirty. I needed a bath. I needed to scrub the sense of death from my skin and warm myself. The cold had seeped into my bones, making me ache in a painful way, every inch of me craving something hot. And while Jameson's body was that and more, I still wanted a bath.

Jameson's kiss gentled when we entered the bathroom, turning soft and sweet. Ending with tiny presses of his lips against mine. Almost refusing to stop.

"I hated seeing you like that," he whispered, his voice rough and his arms shaking. "But when the bond broke…"

I leaned my forehead against his, gripping him, unwilling to let go. "I know. I saw you. It was horrible to not be able to reach you."

"It was too much. The memories…"

"I know." I ran my hand down his cheek. "But you gave me something to come back for."

I held up my hand, his dried blood still staining the lines and wrinkles of my palm. "You kept me grounded on this plane. You were my reason to fight my way home, and I won't ever leave you behind."

"Aoife," he whispered before he kissed me again, his lips warm and soft against mine. "You should rest."

I shook my head slowly, wishing I could dive into the fire in his blue eyes. "I don't really want to rest, do you?"

He growled, fingers clutching at me, almost hurting. I'd certainly have bruises eventually. Not that I minded at all.

"You promised to wash my back," I whispered, my lips against his chin.

He huffed, still shaking. "I'll wash whatever needs washing."

"Then let's get in the tub. I want to be clean before I wrap myself around you in that bed."

He set me down, pressing a kiss to my lips before pulling off his cloak and tossing it into a corner. Once naked, he stepped into the tub, grabbing my hand while lowering himself into the hot water. He kept us connected, kept us touching. I followed him, sitting in between his legs, and leaned back against his chest, pulling his arms around me. Wrapping my legs over his. Craving the physicality, needing every inch of him against me.

The warmth of the water seeped in to replace the cold, the pain inside fading as Jameson and I sat in silence. Enjoying the quiet and the feel of skin on skin. Being together with nothing between us.

"When I was a little girl," I finally started as the water began to cool a bit, "I would talk to these people-shaped flashes that seemed to follow me. I called them my lightdows instead of shadows until I learned not to talk about them at all. Everyone thought I was crazy except Percy. He knew." I ran a washcloth down Jameson's legs, washing him, letting my mind wander as my hands did the same. "They became stronger as I got older. Louder, but more staticky. Harder to hear."

He kissed my shoulder, humming against my skin as I remembered. All that embarrassment, the fear, and the loneliness that came with seeing things no one else could. The false starts and desperate search for answers as to how and why and what to do.

"The ghosts made my life hell for many years, but then I met a lady named Eliza who was just like me. She took me under her wing and taught me what it was to be a necromancer. She made me feel accepted and helped me learn all this gift entailed."

I turned, water splashing over the sides as I straddled him. Leaning against his chest as I kept talking, kept thinking, kept needing him to understand. "The first time I tranced to the land between, I almost didn't make it back because I had no idea what I was doing. Even with Eliza beside me, the lure of the dead was almost too strong to resist. But I've learned. I know how to go from place to place. No one alive is truly safe in the land between, but I always cover my bases to make the trip as easy as possible."

I rocked over him, just once, leaning down to kiss his collarbone, my hands running up and down his chest.

"Aoife," Jameson said, his head tilted back, his body stiff in all the right ways.

"Yes, Jameson?"

"Fucking come back." He grabbed me, pulled me to him, his hand cradling the back of my head so I couldn't move. "I'll lay right beside you in my wolf form if that grounds you more, but you'd better fucking come back. Because I'll hunt you down if you don't. I'll go toe-to-toe with Death if I have to."

I whimpered, leaning forward enough to bite his bottom lip. "You won't have to. I'll be careful. I'll always come back to you."

He hummed, hands releasing me as his lips met mine in a slow, wet kiss. He dragged his knuckles up and down my back before taking one hand further, sliding it over my ass and down, slipping between my legs to tease me.

"Do you feel clean enough yet, beautiful?"

I pressed myself against his fingers, rocking, needing more. "I don't even care anymore."

"Good." Without another word, he stood, water dripping from the two of us as he carried me to the bedroom. I kept my body against his, kept my lips on his neck until he tossed me on the mattress. Soaking wet.

His growly laugh made me smirk, made me feel devious and playful after such a serious moment. So I sprawled in the middle of the bed, planting my feet on the mattress and spreading my knees wide. He jerked, holding his ground but dropping his smile. I sucked one finger into my mouth before trailing it down my body, over my breasts, past my navel, to finally rub over my clit in slow, easy circles. Letting myself enjoy it, letting him watch. And watch he did, with bright eyes and a hearty rumble in his chest, one that made me grow wet and swollen for him. One that made me want more.

He groaned as my hand moved faster, his own going to his cock, grabbing and sliding along the length. I mimicked his motions, following his rhythm, matching his timing. And I waited for him to come to me, to tease me, to make me his again. Until finally, I couldn't wait any longer.

"C'mere, my mate."

NINETEEN

Jameson

GOD, SHE WAS BEAUTIFUL. All pale skin and dark hair with those big eyes that made her look like some kind of sweet fucking fairy. But I knew better. I'd seen the naughty woman living underneath that innocent exterior. I'd felt her come around me, heard the dirty words fall from her lips, tasted her pleasure.

And I was going to do it all again.

I crawled up the mattress, spreading her knees wider with my shoulders, knocking her hand away from what I wanted.

"Mine."

The grumble of that one word made her giggle. She wouldn't be giggling for long, though. I held her open, lifted her ass off the mattress with both hands so I could pull her beautiful pussy to my face, and licked her in one long, wet stripe from back to front. Growling the whole time.

That giggle cut off real quick.

"Jameson."

Her breathy moan of my name was more than enough consent for me. I dove in, tongue flat as I licked her, keeping those legs spread even when she tried to pull them together. I

Claiming His Desire

knew this would be a little much for her, riding that edge of pleasure and pain, but I wanted it. Wanted her. Needed her to feel, to come, to fucking lose her mind on my tongue.

Hands locked in my hair, tugging hard, Aoife gasped and moaned as I continued working her. From long licks of her lips to flicks with the tip of my tongue right on her little clit, I kept her wondering what was next. Kept her writhing as I set her back on the mattress and crawled closer. Arms wrapped under her thighs and around, holding her down, using my thumbs to spread her lips wide.

"Fuck, Aoife. So pink and pretty. I'll never get enough."

I zeroed in on her clit, sealing my lips around it, suckling hard. Aoife practically arched off the bed, twisting and yanking on my hair as she yelled something that didn't quite sound like English. I kept up the pressure, dropping one hand to slide a finger inside. Two. In and out a few times, teasing, then I added a third.

She tried to escape my hold, to back away from my touch. Not that I let her. Sucking her clit, giving her a tiny flick with my tongue every few seconds, fucking her with my hand—I worked her hard. Pushed her body how I wanted. And she fucking loved every second of it. My chin was soaked with the proof.

Repositioning my mouth, I sucked again, steady and strong. Aoife screeched, arms and legs shaking, hands yanking on my hair. Close. So fucking close. Just a little more, a little bit extra. So I bent my three fingers inside of her, catching the top of her pubic bone, holding it. And I pulled down. Not hard, not anything painful, just enough for her to feel that tension. Tongue flat on her clit, I matched the pressure of my fingers, pushing and pulling. And then I growled. Loudly.

Aoife came with a jolt, her entire body seizing, her pussy quivering in a rhythm that left me fighting not to come, milking my fingers, arousal dripping down my hand.

Finally, she shoved me away, squeezing her legs together and cutting me off from my new favorite playground.

"Too much, baby?" I rubbed her thigh, kissed a little beauty mark on her knee.

"Fuck, no." She huffed a laugh, tossing an arm over her face. "But if you kept breathing on me, I was going to come again."

I growled as I slid up her body, keeping as much of my skin in contact with hers as I could. "And why would that be a bad thing?"

She smiled, a naughty burn in her eyes that made my wolf sit up and take notice. Made my cock practically weep for her attention.

"Because I owe you one now, and I always pay my debts."

She twisted, pulling me with her, until I ended up on my back with her on top of me.

"This has potential," I murmured, reaching up and palming her breasts. She arched into my touch with a sigh before pulling away.

"Not yet, big boy."

I thrust my hips up in a slow lift, smirking as she rode me. "Big is the right word."

Aoife laughed, sliding down my body, lying along the length of my legs with her head on my hip. "There are times when you are so sweet and caring, so supportive and kind to me. And then there are times when you are such a dirty boy."

"Only with you." I met her eyes, trying to enhance my words with the truth in my expression. "I'm only that way with you. Every side of me. Out there, they get one Jameson, Feral Breed Jameson. You get all of me."

A smile, so sweet and filled with affection, my heart practically leaped out of my chest. That smile was for me, just me. And I loved it.

"I know."

Eyes on mine, she wrapped her hand around my hard cock. I groaned and pushed into her fist, seeking more, needing it. She kept her grip tight, moving her hand in a slow, stroking motion. Teasing me. Making me growl and shake as she rubbed her thumb in circles over the tip. Used a finger to trace along the underside of the head.

"Fuck, Aoife." I whimpered when she kissed the tip, tongue flicking the head twice before she pulled away again.

"What would you like?"

I glanced down, seeing that naughty fairy again. Growling as she licked that tip one more fucking time. The tease.

So I smirked. "I want you to suck me, Aoife. Wrap those pretty lips around my cock and show me how deep you can go."

Her smile turned wicked, almost proud, and I knew I was in trouble.

Aoife

I TOOK JAMESON INTO my mouth, keeping my gaze locked with his, sliding down his length slow and steady. His eyes were so dark, so hot with need, making me wet for him again. This man… Everything about him turned me on, including the taste of him on my tongue.

As I reached the base, I moaned, letting him feel exactly how deep he was. Jameson's eyes practically rolled back in his head, and he grabbed a fistful of my hair.

"Fuck, Aoife. Fuck…seriously?"

I groaned and pulled almost all the way off him, laving the ridge of his cock with my tongue as I did. I dropped down again. Faster this time. All the way down. Swallowing him deep. His hips bucked, his growl coming steady and loud as I continued my pattern. Up and down, faster on each stroke, letting my tongue tease all the way up. Flicking the underside of the head every few strokes. Lightly dragging my teeth along the underside just to watch him squirm. And squirm he did. Legs pulled up, spread, one hand in my hair, the other on the side of my face, thumb running over my jaw. Fuck, so hot. So mine.

As I sank down again, I slid my hand to cup between his legs. His groan was enough to tell me I was on the right path, so I massaged and tugged, working his balls as I sucked his heavy cock. On an upward pull, I released him from my lips, holding him still. Twisting my hand on his cock to keep him on edge, I sucked a finger from my other hand into my mouth, wetting it. He watched, wide-eyed and breathing hard. When I knew my finger was ready, I slid it down the length of him. Holding his gaze. Dropping my head to take him back in my mouth as my hand slipped past his balls. Down. Farther. Teasing the skin between. Pressing at that place most people ignored.

"Yeah, shit, do that." Jameson jerked, body going rigid, breathing hard as I kept up my rhythm. Up and down, massage the balls, press against the skin behind them. Suck him deep and hard, tease the head. Repeating over and over and—

With no warning, Jameson jackknifed to a sitting position, yanked me up the length of his body, and flipped us. He slid inside me on a single thrust, so fast and hard, it stole my breath.

"Damn it, Jam—" I gasped as he thrust into me again, rougher, deeper, almost making it hurt. "Jesus. I wasn't fucking done."

He bit my bottom lip, eyes wild, growling uncontrollably. "Need to come in your pussy, baby."

Well…damn.

I nodded, barely able to speak, too turned on to make words. Instead, I clung to his shoulders, pushing back against him on every thrust, taking all of him as he lost control. Head in my neck, growling, he fucked me like a man possessed. Like a man who had something to prove. And I took every bit of it. Wrapped myself around him and enjoyed the wet sounds of us coming together. Clung to him as the pressure inside built once more. Until I was seconds from coming.

"Jameson," I gasped when he rotated his hips against mine, punishing my clit in the best way.

He nodded into my neck, understanding my breathy moan, pushing my knees up to his shoulders to change the angle and give me what I needed. More pressure, more depth, more contact between the base of his cock and my clit. And damn, it was good. Three more thrusts and I lost it. Every muscle clenching, eyes closed, coming silently because I had no energy left to scream his name like I wanted to.

And then he bit me.

Like the last time, the pain of his bite receded, leaving nothing but pleasure, making my orgasm resurge through my body. I shook and gasped, clinging to his muscled back, legs wrapped around him as his thrusts grew wilder, jerky, losing rhythm. He pulled his teeth out of me and roared as he came, his entire body stretched, arching up from where we were joined.

When he finally relaxed, licking his lips and breathing hard as his thrusts slowed to lazy shifts of his hips, I snuggled back into his chest, letting him hold me, catching my breath.

"Hey, Jameson?" I asked, kissing his chest, tasting the salt on his skin.

He groaned, sliding out of me but holding me closer yet. "Yeah?"

"I think we're going to need to spend some time way out in the desert."

"Why's that?"

I hitched my leg over his hip, opening myself up to him. Not intentionally, of course. Well, kind of.

"Because I really want to make you roar like that again, and I'm pretty sure my neighbors will call the cops if they hear it."

He hummed, licking his way over my new mating bite and

making me shiver. "I have a little place outside Spring Valley. It's private, quiet, and we can do anything we like without fear of upsetting neighbors. I can take you on the back porch at sunrise, if you want."

"Can you work from there?"

Jameson froze, almost holding his breath. "I'm not going to be working with the Feral Breed anymore, Aoife."

"Yeah, you are," I said, running my hands over his skin. "These people are your friends, your family. Maybe you don't have to go back to doing what you were before, but you need to stay connected to them."

He sighed. "I can't stand the thought of you involved in any of that."

I pulled his face to mine, looking him square in the eye. "I'll be involved simply because you're in my life, but I think we can find a balance if we try to. If you're willing to see me as capable."

"Aoife, I know you're capable." He rolled a bit, pulling me with him. "I'm terrified of losing you, though."

"So we try. We head to your place in the desert, and we see how much involvement we each feel comfortable with. I'll still be helping the dead, Jameson. It's what I do. And you can help your shifter friends because it's what *you* do. There has to be a middle ground between locking me in a room somewhere and me battling shifters with my bare hands. Or my bow. Whichever works best."

Jameson chuckled. "Okay, my little arguer. We'll go to my place, and I'll stay involved with the Feral Breed…for now. We can play it by ear, do a few missions or work at the clubhouse, until we find our comfort level."

I arched into him, pressing my breasts against the planes of his chest. "Sounds perfect."

He rolled to his back until I lay sprawled across him. "It will be once you're there."

"Sweet-talker," I whispered.

He pushed my hair off my face and ran his thumb over my cheek. "Only with you."

I leaned down, kissing him, unable to resist. Knowing this was a moment of change for us. An ending and a beginning. A fresh start to a relationship that had begun over a year ago, that flourished in visions and false memories, that tore us each apart in different ways.

A new lease on our lives.

"Hey, Aoife," Jameson whispered, his hands sliding down to grab my ass.

I moaned, closing my eyes as he kneaded my flesh. "Yeah?"

He leaned close, growling in my ear. "Less thinking, more kissing."

I laughed and pulled him closer. He was right...the time for thinking was over. At least for a little while.

"Anything for you, my mate."

EPILOGUE

Aoife

THE WIND WHISTLED THROUGH the air, soft and light, just enough to cool off the late afternoon heat. The stones of grave markers and crypts jutted from the green grass, all shapes and sizes. Each one carved for a reason, for a person. Perhaps to show the wealth of the deceased or the respect they'd earned in their life, or maybe they were a tribute to the legacy left behind. No matter the reason, they decorated the landscape, a mismatched collection of remembrances of lives long past.

Beautiful and alive, the grass-covered rolling hills welcomed me with a softness that drew me in, made me want to lie back and sleep. The cemetery adjacent to Merriweather Fields had closed an hour before I'd arrived, the caretaker leaving as soon as he'd locked the gates. And while I understood the need for security in places such as this, the fences and obstacles didn't matter to me. The spirits trapped between the living and the dead needed me tonight, and I'd made them a promise. I would listen to their stories and invest the time to help them transition once and for all. It was a huge undertaking, the biggest I'd ever attempted, but I knew it would work. I had faith that I was strong enough to help the ones who truly wanted to go into the land of the dead. And I had the best reasons to return to the land of the living close at hand, just in case the lure of the land between became too much for me.

Quietly, concentrating on the job to be done, I sat in the soft grass and laid out my trinkets. Bones and dead flesh, a lock of hair from the body of a witch named Amber. Something Scarlett had given to me after my trip to the Summerlands. A way to honor the witch who gave her life to protect her friend and ensure the future safety of her sisters. All meaningful and important, all things I respected to my very core.

Bag empty, I sat back to center myself. Dead on my left, right side not quite ready. I no longer needed to carry my living reminders, having found something better. Something that pulled me back faster than all the plants and bits of earth I could hold. Fate and love, hope and faith...all gifts that kept me solidly on the living plane. All things I would forever be grateful for, that I would cling to and care about.

I closed my eyes and took a deep breath, cleansing my soul for the journey to come. Quiet surrounded me, the whisper of the wind the only sound at first. But then a rhythmic pace of large paws on the grassy ground grew near, making my heart beat faster. The warmth of humid breath, the cold touch of a wet nose against my cheek, and then the weight of a fur-covered head landed in my lap. My right hand dropped of its own accord, scratching ears I'd know anywhere.

"Stay with me," I whispered.

He answered with a huff and a crawl closer, more weight in my lap on my right side. His warmth surrounding me, grounding me in this place, creating a link to where I most wanted to be, the person I most wanted to be with. I ran my hand over his head and down, curling my fingers into the fur at his scruff. Holding on with my body. Ready to let go with my soul.

The roar of a group of motorcycles driving down the road,

leaving Merriweather Fields, caused the earth to vibrate subtly underneath me, my mate's growl joining the rumble. People going home, back to their lives and families. Order restored in the world of wolf shifters. At least for now.

Refocusing, I gave myself over to the job at hand. In the warmth of the evening, with my mate by my side, I searched out the realm of the dead. Knowing I'd make it back. Clinging to the neck of a wolf as my guide. Ready to help those who couldn't help themselves.

And then I called to the cold, to the dead…let myself fall into a trance. Fulfilling one final promise before Jameson and I left to begin our lives anew in Arizona. Before seeking the stability we'd been craving all our lives. Man and wolf. Living and dead. Jameson and Aoife. Two halves of the same whole. Joined by fate, tied with blood, balanced in love.

Forever.

A frightened shifter trapped inside herself.

A man tired of living a life in the dark.

A fate worth waiting for.

CLAIMING HER HEART

FERAL BREED MOTORCYCLE CLUB
BOOK SEVEN

ACKNOWLEDGMENTS

This is the last book in what I call "The Hunt for the Omegas" plot. It's also the one I've been waiting to write from the start. Jameson and I have spent a lot of time together in my head, much like he and his Aoife (though not as dirty...promise). And though many things have changed over the course of the last year or so—plot twists and characters popping up in the most unusual of ways— Jameson has remained true. He was always a man who was done with life, suffering from the grief of losing what he never truly had. I'm happy Aoife popped up (because she wasn't planned... at all) and saved him from spiraling into the dark. I read a saying once - "When you get to the bottom of your rope, tie a knot." The missing Omegas were Jameson's knot, giving him a handhold until his mate resurrected herself.

There aren't enough words to thank my friend and editor, Lisa Hollett. From day one, she's been behind me, making sure I put out the best books I can and keeping me from self-destructing under the pressure of this business (even when that meant simply sending snacks and whiskey). I'm thankful for her and can't wait to see where our adventures take us next. (Alaska? Las Vegas? Scotland?)

To Caren, Esher, and Anna, who jump in with advice and cheerleading whenever I need them. Critique partners, especially good ones, are worth their weight in gold. These ladies are worth even more to me.

To my friends, my readers, and my family...your love and support inspire me in ways you may never truly know. Thanks for going on this journey with me.

ABOUT THE AUTHOR

A storyteller from the time she could talk, Ellis grew up among family legends of hauntings, psychics, and love spanning decades. Those stories didn't always have the happiest of endings, so they inspired her to write about real life, real love, and the difficulties therein. From farmers to werewolves, store clerks to witches—if there's love to be found, she'll write about it. Ellis lives in the Chicago area with her husband, daughters, and a giant dog who hogs the bed.

Find Ellis online at:
Website: www.ellisleigh.com
Twitter: https://twitter.com/ellis_writes
Facebook: https://www.facebook.com/ellisleighwrites

Edited by Silently Correcting Your Grammar, LLC
Cover Art by Cormar Covers